RUINS OF FATE

THE OMNI TOWERS SERIES PREQUEL

JAMIE A. WATERS

Ruins of Fate © 2019 by Jamie A. Waters

Cover Art by Deranged Doctor Designs
Editor: Beyond DEF Lit

ISBN: 978-1-949524-12-3 (Hardback Edition)
ISBN: 978-1-949524-02-4 (Paperback Edition)
ISBN: 978-1-949524-03-1 (eBook Edition)

Library of Congress Control Number: 2019902597
First Edition *April 2019

THE OMNI TOWERS SERIES

Ruins of Fate

Ruins of Fate
Beneath the Fallen City
Shadow of the Coalition
Tremors of the Past
Drop of Hope
Flames of Redemption
Spirit of the Towers

CHAPTER ONE

THE WIND HOWLED, its eerie scream reminiscent of a death wail that could be heard through the tight fit of Skye's helmet. Goose bumps pebbled her skin beneath the protective UV jacket she wore, but she pushed aside her misgivings. Instead, she reached for another handhold and continued to climb the steep roof's edge.

The gathering dark clouds seemed desperate to avoid the strange green light that cast itself over the sky above her. A lightning bolt streaked out with spiderweb-like tendrils, encouraging Skye to climb even faster, and distant thunder rumbled its warning a few seconds later. She felt the reverberations through her gloved hands as she gripped another handhold. It wasn't too much farther, but she needed to hurry. The storm was moving quicker than they'd anticipated.

She tried to push off her foothold, but her boot broke through the rotted support. Mentally swearing at her miscalculation, she gripped tightly to the edge she was holding and yanked her foot free. The clatter of debris falling downward was a reminder she needed to be more careful. This whole roof would collapse soon, and she'd rather not be on top of it when it did.

Scanning the roof, Skye tried to look for dips which might indicate more rot. Attempting to avoid them, she used her feet and arms to propel herself toward the top of the sloping roof. Between the relentless wind and the dilapidated condition of the building, her odds were a little less than fair. If she managed to survive, she'd probably have an entertaining story to share with her camp later—she just had to make sure she lived long enough to tell it.

A man's voice came over her earpiece, "You okay, Skye? Do you need me to come out there and show you how it's done?"

Despite the precariousness of the situation, Skye grinned at the sound of her scavenging partner's voice. Reaching for another handhold, she pulled herself up even higher. "Aw, Leo. You couldn't catch me if you tried."

Chance guffawed. "She's got you there. Besides, her ass looks better climbing up that roof than yours ever will."

"Can't argue that," Leo agreed.

"I'm flattered," she said, avoiding another area of the roof that was likely ready to collapse. "If I had known watching my ass was enough to get you both off yours, I would have handled the past few years differently."

Leo chuckled. "You're almost to the top. See if you can get a sight on our communication equipment."

"So bossy," she muttered but continued climbing. At the top of the ridgeline, Skye straddled the edge and looked toward the apex of the roof. The lookout was a rudimentary construct they'd designed months earlier to mount their communication equipment. Unfortunately, the condition of the building and their lack of resources made it fail more often than not.

She sighed. "Well, shit. You want the good news or the bad news?"

"Bad," Leo said over her earpiece.

"Looks like the antenna's broken. I can't tell if it's repairable from here. I'm going to have to climb the whole way."

"And the good news?" Chance prompted.

"You get to stare at my ass a bit longer."

Chance chuckled, and Skye carefully made her way toward the lookout. The only good thing was that the ridgeline was in a bit better shape than other less reinforced areas of the roof, but it made her more of a target for the elements.

A gust of wind threatened to knock her off the roof, and she flattened herself, trying to make herself as small of a target as possible.

So much for Chance and Leo's view of my ass.

Continuing to inch forward on her stomach, Skye let out a sigh of relief when she reached the edge of the lookout. The wall offered a bit of shelter from the impending storm, but she'd need to hurry before the skies opened up.

The antenna had snapped almost completely in half, with only the barest attachment remaining. That explained their loss of communication to the outlying areas and their scavenging crews in the ruins. If they lost the full piece of metal, it wouldn't be easy to replace—not to mention the danger to all their campmates if they couldn't warn them about the approaching storm.

Gripping the edge of the lookout with her gloved hands, Skye pulled herself up to the top. The wind was even worse up here, and the slightest miscalculation would send her tumbling to the ground. Reaching out, she tried to catch the antenna as it whipped through the air. Her fingers touched it, causing it to snap off the rest of the way.

Dammit.

On the plus side, they hadn't lost the piece. But Daryl, their camp leader, was going to be less than pleased when he learned they needed to replace the entire thing. Doing her best to ignore the wind beating against her, Skye gripped the broken piece of metal and base of the antenna. Holding the two together, she began to wind some metallic-fusion tape around them. They didn't have much tape left, and she needed to be careful not to waste any of their precious supply. No one knew when they'd be able to afford to buy more from one of the Omni trading camps.

Through the static on her headset, she could barely make out the sound of Leo's gravelly voice. "Hurry, Skye. The storm's going to be here any minute. We're already getting local interference."

"Patience, handsome. This girl likes to be finessed first," she said, pulling out her knife and cutting off the end of the tape to seal the edges shut. It wasn't much of a hold, but their options were limited. "Okay. Try reaching them now."

"Switching channels."

Skye waited, continuing to hold the antenna in place as she watched the ominous clouds moving overhead. Getting caught on the roof in an electrical storm was one of the last things she needed, but if they didn't get communication reestablished with their crews scavenging in the ruins, more lives than just hers would be at risk.

From her location perched on the roof, she could barely make out the Omni Towers in the distance. No matter how bad the storms became, they never seemed to affect the self-sustaining facility. While most of the world had been ravaged during the last war almost two centuries earlier, OmniLab had remained virtually untouched. She'd only seen the towers up close one time, the barest touch of a life so far removed from her own that it was nearly unfathomable.

Thousands of people lived within the Omni Towers, but

few would ever deign to step outside their walls. Like most ruin rats or surface-dwellers, she'd grown up hearing fanciful stories about OmniLab and life within the towers. But that's all they were—stories. Few people knew the truth and the ones who did refused to talk. Those not born in the towers were never allowed to walk their halls.

Lightning streaked across the sky again, followed almost immediately by a rumble of thunder. Skye continued to watch the dark clouds moving overhead as she tried to bury her unease and mentally willed Leo to hurry. The hazards of her current rooftop perch would become even worse once the rain started to fall.

A strange chill went through her that had nothing to do with the temperature dropping. If the skies were any indication, this storm would be worse than any other in recent history. It was more than the storm though. It was as though the elements themselves were threatening to unleash their full fury upon the already battered world. Some primal part of her understood that something was coming, and this storm was just the beginning.

Chance's voice broke through her thoughts. "Well, now that I have you all to myself on this channel, let's talk about how I can get you alone back at camp..."

Skye grinned, not terribly upset by the distraction. Chance's teasing banter was a welcome diversion. There was no real heat behind it, although she was sure he wouldn't be opposed to spending some time together if she indicated her interest. But that wouldn't ever happen.

"Daryl's gonna toss your ass over the side of the roof if you finish that thought on a public channel, Chance."

"Damn. He's probably monitoring too," Chance grumbled.

"Yes, he is," Daryl interrupted. "Get off this channel and

stay off unless it's important. You want to get laid? Do it on your own time."

Skye's smile deepened, and she shook her head in exasperation. Their camp leader frequently seemed to be lacking a sense of humor. He knew his stuff though, which was part of the reason their camp was more successful than many other scavenging camps.

Leo's voice came over her headset again. "Dammit. No good. The storm's interfering too much. Get off that roof, Skye. We'll have to hope they find shelter and can wait until the storm passes."

She frowned and stared up at the sky. They all knew what could happen to their people if they didn't get a message to them warning them to get to safety. Steeling herself, she pushed up from her crouched position on the roof and tried to brace herself against the angry wind. Skye held the antenna with both hands and shouted, "Not a chance, Leo. Try now."

She barely heard his curse before he was gone. The wind whipped around her wildly, threatening to toss her from the rooftop and shatter her body with its relentless force. She gritted her teeth, trying to keep her feet planted against the onslaught. Clutching the antenna tightly, she held it into the air like a weapon and challenged the heavens with her defiance.

"Hurry, Leo," she urged, unsure how long she could keep holding on. In a battle against the elements, she was no match against them. "Getting fried up here isn't my idea of a good time."

The wind beat against her, and their makeshift antenna would snap completely if it picked up much more. If they didn't warn their people about the approaching storm, a dozen people might become trapped within the ruins where they were scavenging.

The buildings they were searching for tradable materials

were already crumbling and in severe disrepair. Another storm like the one approaching could be enough to collapse a building on top of them—or worse. They'd lost another crew member when a support structure fell on him during a storm several months ago. They couldn't afford to lose anyone else.

Another gust of wind kicked up, throwing her off balance. The antenna whipped out of her hand and she fell backward, tumbling off the edge of the lookout and onto the roof. A scream ripped out of her throat. Skye scrambled, grabbing at anything to stop her rapid descent as she slid down the roof and toward the ground.

Her fingers brushed against an exposed metal beam, and she bit back a curse as the jagged edge cut through her gloves and into the meat of her hands. Grabbing it, she struggled against the pain to hold on. The roof underneath her boots gave way and fell inward. She gripped the beam tightly, trying desperately to pull herself back up.

"Skye!" Leo shouted over her headset.

Reaching out with her other hand, Skye tried to find purchase on the roof. Her feet flailed, but there was nothing beneath her. Between her angle and the slope of the roof, it was impossible to pull herself back up.

"I can't hold on, Leo," she managed, trying to suppress the panic rising inside her. She couldn't die. Not like this.

"Baby, I'm almost there," he urged. "I see you. Just a few more seconds."

She looked up, watching as Leo slid down the side of the roof. He shouldn't have come after her, but it didn't stop her relief at seeing him. He was too heavy for the roof, but at least he had one of the temporary harnesses they used for scavenging. It would hopefully keep him from falling like she had.

Her hand was starting to go numb from the metal cutting into it, but she fought to hold on. Leo's foot broke through the roof, but he managed to catch himself and continued inching toward her.

Leo laid down on the roof, spreading out his body weight. Grabbing her jacket, he hauled her up enough so she could pull herself up the rest of the way. Another gust of wind threatened to knock them over again. Skye flattened herself, trying to make herself less of a target for the storm.

"Dammit. I think I ruined my gloves."

"To hell with your gloves!" Leo shouted over the headset. "The whole roof is starting to collapse. This building won't make it through the storm. We've got to move. Can you climb with that hand?"

"I don't have much of a choice," she said, determined to avoid looking at her hand. Right now, the adrenaline was numbing the pain, but she knew if she saw the damage, her brain would suddenly release how much it hurt. The mind was tricky like that.

Leo started to unhook the cable around his waist. "Chance, get ready to pull her up."

Her gaze flew to Leo's. "No! Chance, hold."

"What the fuck am I doing up here?" Chance snapped. "Make a decision *now*. That cable won't support both of you, and we've already lost the northeast quadrant of the roof."

"I'm more graceful than you, Leo, even if I'm hurt," Skye argued, unwilling to voice her true fears. She couldn't allow him to sacrifice himself for her. "I'll race you back to the ladder."

Leo cursed and reattached the cable around his waist. He pulled her close, clutching her tightly, and said, "You're a fucking lousy liar. Go ahead and climb, but I'm not leaving your side."

Skye nodded. Leo was always as good as his word. It was one of the reasons she trusted him implicitly as her scavenging partner. Getting into a crawling position, she tested the roof for weakness before she crept forward. It was an agonizingly slow progress, but every second took them closer to safety.

They'd installed a ladder on the side of the building to access their antenna and communication equipment. It was the tallest building in the area, and it gave them the best range to keep in contact with their campmates scavenging in the ruins. Now that this building was falling, they'd need to find another location to mount their equipment. But those worries would need to come later, relocating the equipment would be someone else's problem if she didn't survive the next few hours.

Another peal of thunder caused the building to shake, and the skies opened up a moment later. Rain beat down on them, making the surface even more treacherous. Skye's foot slipped, but Leo caught her before she could fall again. She tried to push herself back up to a crawl position, but her hand wouldn't support her weight. Dammit. The numbing effects of the adrenaline was starting to wear off.

Through her headset, Leo said, "Move your ass, Skye. We need to get off this roof."

"Everyone's obsessed with my ass today," she muttered, using her elbows to crawl the rest of the way.

Chance waited at the top of the ladder with the cabling device. A small ledge had been mounted off the side of the roof, and it was already swaying from the combination of their weight and the storm.

"One of you needs to start cutting back on your rations," she said, gripping the edge of the platform tightly. "It's a little crowded up here."

Leo unhooked the cable from his harness. "Chance could stand to miss a few meals."

Chance snorted and quickly secured the equipment and

started climbing down the rickety ladder. "I know when I'm not wanted. See you surface-side, kids."

Skye crouched on the ledge next to Leo, waiting for Chance to reach the ground. The ladder was flimsy, and they couldn't all risk climbing down at the same time. She watched Chance descend until he disappeared from her view. It was a long way down.

A few minutes later, Chance's voice came over the head-set. "I'm on the ground."

Leo turned toward her. "Can you make it down the ladder?"

"With one hand tied behind my back," Skye retorted, not willing to discuss her injuries until they were safe. Knowing Leo, he'd put himself at risk again to protect her. "You should go first, Leo. You're too heavy on this ledge. I'm thinking Chance isn't the only one who's been double dipping on the food rations."

Leo hesitated. Skye gripped his arm with her good hand. "Go. I can make it. If I fall, you'll catch me."

"Don't even joke about that shit," Leo growled but moved toward the ladder.

Skye sat back on her heels, watching him descend. The rain was making it even more difficult to see. She wiped her visor with her gloved hand, but it did little good. She lost sight of Leo about halfway down. Even through her helmet, she could hear the groaning of the building as the storm beat upon it.

"Go ahead, Skye," Leo said over her headset.

Skye positioned herself in front of the ladder. Hooking her arm through the rungs, she started her shaky descent. Each step down, she'd have to grip the ladder tightly with her good hand, hook her injured arm through the next rung, and take another step. It was painstakingly slow, and the rain was beginning to seep through her clothing. Her teeth chattered from the pain in her injured hand and the chill in the wind.

"Talk to me, Skye."

"I'm more than halfway, Leo," she managed, taking another step.

A resounding *crash* filled the air, and Chance shouted over the headset, "We just lost the rear of the building! The whole thing's about to go down. Hurry your ass up."

Skye took him at his word and continued moving. The ladder wobbled underneath her, and her breath hitched as it began sliding away from the building. Her arm was still hooked under one of the rungs, and she held on, mentally willing it to stop moving.

"Hold the fucking ladder!" Leo ordered. "Skye, I'm coming back up for you."

"No!" she yelled. "You'll collapse it. Just stay the hell down there."

"She's right," Chance said, his voice tinged with worry. "Come on, Skye. We're trying to hold it steady."

"I'd appreciate you doing a bit better than trying," she retorted. "I thought you liked me, Chance."

"I do, but I'm starting to think *you're* the one who needs to cut back on her rations."

"Payback's gonna hurt," she promised, moving down another rung, and then another.

It was tempting to rush even more, but she knew from experience that even worse accidents could happen from the slightest miscalculation. Panic was never your friend in these types of situations. It wouldn't matter how much they were holding on to the ladder if the whole building came down— she'd be an ugly smear on the ground either way.

"Gotta get your ass down here first," Chance reminded her. "Your threats don't mean shit when you're hanging in the air."

Skye heard a screeching groan and another loud *crash*. A cloud of dust billowed up from somewhere nearby. Another floor must have collapsed, but it was closer this time. Not even the downpour was minimizing the impact of the building falling apart. Her heart thudded in her chest as she continued to descend. It was almost impossible to see the ground between the construction dust and the rain obstructing her vision.

Focusing on her movements, she moved down another step and hooked her arm through the next rung. The ladder began shaking violently, and she clung to it tightly as it started to tilt backward.

"Drop, Skye!" Leo shouted. "The wall's going."

Trusting Leo at his word, Skye squeezed her eyes shut and pushed back from the ladder. For a second, she was suspended in midair before plummeting downward.

CHAPTER TWO

SKYE CRASHED INTO LEO, knocking him backward onto the ground. The jarring impact was enough to steal her breath. She rolled over, staring up at the dark clouds as the rain continued to fall. It was a glorious sight and would be even better once she could breathe.

Hopefully, that would happen soon. They needed to get out of the storm before their protective gear was completely ruined from the high acid levels in the rain.

"That was a little too close. You scared the shit out of me. Are you hurt?" Leo propped himself up and leaned over her, running his hand over her jacket and searching for injuries.

Still trying to catch her breath, she focused on moving each of her limbs to make sure nothing was broken. Her bruises were going to have bruises at this rate, but there didn't seem to be any permanent damage. When she could finally speak again, she said, "Just my pride. Let's go."

Leo stood and helped her up. He wrapped his arm around her, pulling her against him. "Chance, grab the cabling gear and let's get inside. This storm's going to get worse before it gets better."

"On it," he said, bending down to lift the equipment.

Leo led Skye back into the building where they'd temporarily set up their camp. They'd been living here for the past several months while they scavenged in some of the nearby ruins. This building was run-down like most others, but they'd been able to excavate the rooms enough to use for their own purposes. They'd formed a suitable shelter to house the almost two dozen people living within the ruin rat camp by using a combination of salvaged building materials from the surrounding areas.

It was one of the better scavenging camps, but it was still a far cry from the more opulent conditions within the OmniLab trading camps. Most of their possessions were cast-offs the trading camps didn't need or use anymore. They'd chosen a location fairly close to the ruins of the fallen cities, which allowed them easier access to trade for critical supplies. The only problem was that those particular ruins were in OmniLab territory, which was more than a little dangerous.

While the trading camps might barter with them for artifacts they'd scavenged in the ruins, the official Omni traders didn't look too favorably upon the ruin rats stealing from their districts. But need for critical supplies had made thievery a necessity. It was possible to get tradable materials from areas farther away, but the cost in time and resources to travel back and forth made it nearly impossible. As it was, their camp was barely able to survive—and they were considered fortunate compared to many others living in the outlying areas.

Skye ducked under a low-hanging beam and into the building. They'd set up a few lights to illuminate some of the areas, but they had tight restrictions about when they could be used. Their solar cells tended to break down more often than not, so power was mostly reserved for critical life-support items. Lights weren't one of them.

Leo helped her pull off her helmet and hung it up on a nearby rack before taking off his own. He ran a hand distractedly through his short dark hair before pulling off the rest of his well-worn protective gear. She fell silent, watching his quick and efficient movements.

Leo was several inches taller than Skye, but sometimes it felt like much more. He had a way of commanding the attention of everyone in a room. Skye would be lying if she said she wasn't drawn to him for more reasons than his considerable skill as a scavenger. He'd captivated her from almost the first moment she'd met him. Meeting Leo had changed everything for her, and he was just as protective of her as she was of him.

He hung up his wet UV jacket, and she noticed it was starting to look a little worn. The patch on his elbow was fraying again and appeared in danger of falling off. She made a mental note to see if they could find something with which to mend it. Things always seemed to break down faster than they could fix them, and Leo tended to put other people's needs before his.

Leo turned back to face her and lifted her injured hand. Her heart beat just a little quicker and not just because the injury was painful. His touch was gentle, and he frowned as he studied her hand.

"We're going to have to cut off the glove."

Skye wrinkled her nose, suspecting he was right. It was doubtful their creative ruin rat engineering would be enough to save it. She'd had this pair of gloves for years, dating back from a time before she'd come to live in the scavenging camp.

"Let's remove the rest of the gear and take a closer look. Maybe we can salvage part of it."

Footsteps sounded from behind her, and she turned to see

Chance dragging in the cabling device. He dropped it on the ground and pulled off his helmet.

"That was a little too close. This storm's going to be a bad one. We'll be lucky if it doesn't take out this building too. Either way, should be an exciting night."

"See if you can help Alanza finish securing the building," Leo suggested, reaching forward to help pull off Skye's jacket. Like the rest of her clothing, it was patched to the point where very little of the original material remained. Unfortunately, that meant the cold rain had seeped under her clothing to cling to her skin. Her teeth chattered, and Leo put his arm around her.

He briskly rubbed her arms to warm her up. "Come on. Let's go in the other room where there's a bit more light. I want to see the damage."

"Next time you decide to undress me, let's try to make it under more enjoyable circumstances," she grumbled, leaning into his warmth as he led her down the hall of the ruin rat camp.

Leo chuckled and squeezed her shoulder. "Then let's get that hand fixed. Next time I undress you, I'm going to want both your hands on me."

"I knew you had an ulterior motive," she teased lightly, stepping around a pile of rubble. They'd cleared a lot of the debris from the building, but some areas of the structure were completely uninhabitable. Space wasn't the problem; they'd only taken over a small portion of it. It was keeping adequate resources in the usable areas that was the tricky part.

Leo led her into one of the rooms where they'd set up their communication and computer systems. A couple of people were working on various things, but one person in particular caught her attention.

"Mom," Veridian called out and rushed over to her. He

wrapped his arms around her and hugged her tightly. Using her good hand, she lightly tousled his hair.

"Hey, little man," she murmured, pressing a kiss against the top of his head. "Staying out of trouble?"

He frowned and looked up at her with eyes that were far older than his seven years. Sometimes, Veridian looked so much like his father, she had trouble seeing any of herself in him. His brown hair and eyes contrasted sharply to her blond hair and blue eyes, but when he smiled, Skye caught sight of the same dimples she possessed. Unfortunately, he didn't smile as often as she'd like.

"You're hurt," he said pointedly, staring at her hand.

"This? Aw, it's just a scratch. Nothing much to worry about."

Leo made a small noise of agreement. "Your mom's tough. She took a hit, but we're going to fix it up. Why don't you get a list of everyone in the field who's checked in? We're going to need their locations once the storm lets up."

When Veridian hesitated, Skye added, "It's important, V. We need to make sure everyone's safe. Go find out from Alanza where everyone's holed up. Then maybe you can help Chance finish strapping down the supplies and secure the building."

Veridian nodded and ran from the room. Skye turned toward Leo. "Thanks for that. He does better when he stays busy."

"He's a good kid," Leo replied.

Walking over to a nearby table, he angled one of their few lights to shine onto it. Skye followed him and sat on a crate, placing her injured hand palm side up on the tabletop. Leo pulled out a knife and began cutting the glove off as close to the seam as possible.

"Niko, grab me the bandages and the healing salve," Leo ordered without looking away from her hand.

Skye winced as he started peeling the glove away from her skin. It felt like Leo was tearing off layers of her skin along with her glove. Now that the adrenaline had worn off, the pain was sharp and vibrant. Her stomach lurched, and she tried to focus on breathing through the worst of it.

Niko, one of the camp's scavengers, brought over a small first aid kit. Like Skye and Leo, he'd been off the scavenging rotation that day and working in camp. They were all scheduled to go back into the ruins tomorrow, but none of them knew if that was going to happen with this storm approaching.

Niko opened the kit. "We ran out of the healing salve last week. I don't think we have many other supplies left."

Skye remained quiet. Medical supplies were the most expensive items to purchase from OmniLab. It wasn't unheard of for some people to try to steal supplies from other camps because of the critical need. It had only served to foster more distrust between those living on the surface. No one knew if the next visitor would have honorable intentions or not—until it was too late. Thankfully, their camp numbers were large enough that they were able to keep people on guard around the clock to watch for any possible intruders.

Until they knew the condition of their people after being trapped in the storm, she wasn't willing to use up their remaining supplies. Any of them could have far more serious injuries. It might be weeks or even months before they were able to replenish their supply cache.

Leo reached into the first aid kit and muttered a colorful curse as he dug around in it. He picked up a vial and shook it, but from the loud rattle, it was almost empty too. "How much pain are you in?"

Skye shook her head. "Just wrap it. I can deal with the pain."

Leo studied her for a long time. She narrowed her eyes at him, and he sighed.

"Stubborn woman," he muttered, placing the vial back in the kit. He lifted her hand again, tilting it toward the light. "Can you move your fingers for me?"

She wiggled her fingers a fraction. It was excruciating, but her hand was still functional. At least she had that going for her. "Looks like I won't be giving Chance the finger for a while."

Niko frowned. "It looks bad, Skye. Maybe Daryl can try to barter with OmniLab for something."

"Nah, I've had worse scrapes," she said, trying to assess the injury with a critical eye.

The nausea rose quickly and suddenly, and she closed her eyes again to focus on her breathing until it passed. It was bad, but it could always be worse. Such an injury would eventually heal, but nerve damage and infection were the biggest threats. At least she was able to move her fingers. The fact she was still bleeding would also help flush out some of the debris and bacteria—she hoped.

Leo was quiet for a long time before gesturing toward the door. "Niko, why don't you go run interference with the kid? I need to clean the wound, and I don't want him coming back in here until it's done."

Niko nodded and headed out of the room.

Skye managed a teasing smile. "You trying to get me alone?"

"Always." Leo chuckled and moved closer. He placed his hand on her knee, his expression more serious. "All joking aside, Niko's right, baby. That wound needs to be treated. We only have a little bit of the wound sealer left. After I clean it, I can close up the worst of it, but we need to try to barter with OmniLab. Otherwise, you'll be out of commission for weeks. I know you're hurting a lot more than you're trying to let on."

Skye blew out a breath. Their camp leader wouldn't be happy if they asked him to make such an exchange on her behalf. She was already in debt for several other concessions he'd made for her. "Just seal it. I'll make do."

He hesitated, and she lifted her gaze to look into Leo's worried eyes. The clear blue color had always revealed the emotion he mostly kept hidden from the world. He only showed that part of himself to her, but even that was rare. It melted her heart a little to know how concerned he was for her welfare.

"Hey, don't get all serious on me," she said and scooted forward. "You know we can't afford it. We don't know how long this storm is going to keep all of us out of work. Besides, I'd rather not ask Daryl for more favors right now."

Leo brushed some of her loose hair away from her face, trailing his fingers across her cheek. "I'll seal it for now, but I want you to promise me you'll let me know if it gets worse."

She stared down at the injury and frowned. Knowing Leo, she probably wouldn't have to say a word. He'd most likely end up checking it every day himself. Sometimes, he worried about her too much.

When she didn't respond, Leo tilted up her chin to meet his gaze. "Don't fuck around with this, Skye. I want your word, or I'll drag your ass to the nearest trading camp right now."

Skye placed her good hand over his and squeezed it gently. She'd tell him, if not for her sake then for her son's. "You have it. I'll tell you if it gets bad."

Leo's shoulders relaxed at her agreement. As much as he denied it, Leo was a wonderful man. Better than she probably deserved, but he was right. She'd do whatever was necessary to make sure she stayed around to look after Veridian.

Leo reached into the medical kit to pull out the wound sealer and began sorting through the rest of the supplies. His movements were efficient and brisk, but she knew a softer side to him. He was much more compassionate than most people realized. Since she'd found her way to Daryl's camp almost eight years ago, Leo had made it his mission to look after her and Veridian, even though neither one of them were his responsibility.

"I'm not particularly happy you took such a risk," he said, placing a hydrating pack and cloth beside her.

She smiled. "You would have done the same if you had been up there."

He scowled but didn't argue the point. "Don't think those dimples of yours are going to get you out of trouble with me."

Skye bit her lip, her smile deepening despite the pain. "They've worked well so far."

Leo paused, his eyes softening as he gazed at her. "I wish I could keep a smile on your face all the time, baby." He reached over to take her injured hand in his, cradling it gently. "Will you close your eyes for me?"

Skye did as he asked and squeezed her eyes shut, bracing herself for the pain. A sharp prick stabbed through her arm, and her eyes flew open. She slapped her hand over the injection site and scowled at the device he was dropping back into the kit.

"What the fuck, Leo? Daryl's going to kill me if he finds out you used our last metabolic booster."

"A dozen people have a chance to survive another day because of what you did tonight," Leo retorted, his expression hardening. "I'll tell Daryl I didn't give you the option. If we're going to have a chance of replenishing our healing supplies quickly, I'm going to need you working at full capacity. We don't know what kind of condition the rest of the crew will be in once they make it back here."

Her jaw clenched, and she glared at him.

Leo sighed. "I can't lose you, Skye. You're one of the few things in this world that's beautiful and good. I'd do anything to keep you safe."

All her anger slipped away, and her throat went dry at the intensity in his expression. "Leo, I... You can't... Dammit. Don't you dare make me cry."

He leaned forward, brushing a kiss against her lips. The pressure was featherlight, but there was an unyielding strength in his kiss. "If you cry, they'll just think you can't handle a little pain. Everyone will know you're not as tough as you pretend."

"That's just mean," she said with a scowl and tried to swat at him with her good hand.

He chuckled, catching her hand before she could make contact. "You can make me pay for it once you're better." His expression sobered. "One day, when I'm running the camp, we're going to do things differently. We'll figure out a way to stop living like this. I'm going to keep you and Veridian safe. You'll see."

Skye frowned. "Don't make promises you can't keep."

Leo smiled, running his thumb over her good hand. "I intend to keep all my promises to you, baby."

The earnestness in his expression made her heart skip a beat. She wanted to believe him, more than anything, but promises were as incandescent as dreams. Hope, however, was nourishment for the soul. Sometimes, that was all the sustenance they could afford.

Skye leaned forward and kissed him lightly. "You're going to be a great camp leader one day."

"With you by my side to kick my ass when I screw up, yeah," he agreed and picked up the cloth. "I need to go ahead and clean the wound. Are you ready? It's going to hurt."

Taking a steadying breath, she nodded. "Yeah. Let's do it."

CHAPTER THREE

THE BUILDING SHOOK as another crack of thunder interrupted the sound of the torrential rain beating against the roof. Skye wiped her brow with her arm and waded through ankle-deep water into the room they'd been using for storage. The storm had already flooded the lower areas of the building, but it was now threatening some of the more critical areas of the camp.

With a wave, she said, "A little more light over here, V."

The light swung back toward her, and she motioned for him to hold it steady. Veridian was standing outside the door, holding up a portable light to illuminate the darkened room. She bent down, trying to identify the labels on the different containers. Their priority was to get the electronic equipment off the ground. Most of the other supplies in this room could handle a little stormwater.

Alanza motioned toward a stack of containers. "Found it. It's over here."

Skye nodded and made her way toward the dark-haired woman. Reaching down, she tried to ignore the sharp pain in her injured hand as she helped stack the heavy containers higher to avoid the rising water.

"If it gets much higher, there won't be much we can do except swim," Alanza muttered and blew out a breath. "What are the chances we're going to get any sleep tonight?"

"Really? You could sleep through this?" Skye winced at the pain as she waded back toward the hallway where Veridian waited. Sleep sounded wonderful, but they couldn't risk it while the water was still rising. Until the storm started to dissipate, they'd all need to stay alert.

Alanza trudged behind her, the sound of splashing water marking her progress. "I'd be willing to try if I didn't have to worry about drowning in my sleep. What do you think, V?"

Veridian frowned and lifted the light higher as they approached. "No way. Chance and Leo might need our help."

Alanza grinned at him and winked. "Even the youngest of us knows better than to sleep through a storm. Guess we're all gonna stay up tonight."

Skye tousled Veridian's hair and reached over to take the light from him, inhaling sharply as the handle made contact with her injury.

Alanza frowned and reached for the light. "I've got it. Did you pull it open again while lifting the crates?"

Skye glanced down at her bandaged hand. "Not sure. I don't want to unwrap it until we get things under control here. It's fine for right now."

Alanza nodded, brushing her dark, curly hair away from her face. The light she carried cast a warm glow over her dusky skin. "You might not want to mention to Leo that you were helping me move the supply crates. He's not going to be happy."

"Probably not," Skye admitted with a sigh, knowing Alanza was downplaying it. "He'd be even less happy if our supplies get ruined though."

Alanza made a noncommittal noise as they headed down the hall. "I don't know about that. I think we could lose just about everything and he'd bounce back as long as you're okay." With a mischievous grin, she added, "I swear, that man is crazy about you."

Skye smiled but didn't respond. Veridian was listening to their conversation a little too closely, and she didn't want to talk about Leo in front of him. Neither she nor Leo had ever publicly advertised how they felt about each other. In fact, they'd agreed to keep their feelings quiet.

Daryl had always gone out of his way to discourage relationships within his camp, claiming it was better to be free of any emotional entanglements. He had a point, but Skye had never been very good at shutting off her emotions simply because it wasn't a good idea. As it was, she and Leo had danced around each for several years before finally admitting what had been growing between them from the start. It was impossible to live and work beside Leo without falling for him.

A loud *crash* interrupted her thoughts, and the entire building trembled. Grabbing Veridian's hand, Skye dashed down the corridor toward where the sound had originated. She stopped short just outside Daryl's office where they'd moved some of their other supplies when the storm had begun. From the brief glimpse through the doorway, the ceiling had started to collapse, most likely from the weight of the water on the roof.

Daryl shouted instructions to whomever was inside the room, "Grab what supplies you can. Niko, find something we can use to seal this room until the storm's over."

Veridian looked up at her. "I can help, Mom."

Skye shook her head and pulled him back, unwilling to let him venture into a room that had already started to collapse. "We need to stay out of the way. Let's go help Niko while they're pulling out supplies. There are some sandbags by the entrance."

Alanza moved forward and put her hand on Skye's arm. "Let me take him, Skye. You know what supplies we need to get out of there."

Skye nodded, motioning for Veridian to go with the other woman. Alanza was right; Skye and Leo were the ones who usually tracked the camp's inventory. Alanza had been like to sister to her for several years, and Skye knew she'd keep a close eye on Veridian. If any other part of the building came down, Skye trusted few others to look out for Veridian the same way she would.

Skye rushed forward into the room where the elements were battling. The UV guard that protected the building was still intact, but it didn't diminish the effects from the storm. Her hair whipped around her face, and she caught the strong metallic scent of ozone in the electrically charged air.

The ceiling had mostly fallen inward, with building debris scattered everywhere. A large hole exposed the darkened sky as rain continued to pour downward. Leo, Chance, and Daryl were working together to secure the supplies and equipment. It was possible some of them could be saved, but the more delicate components had likely already been destroyed by the ceiling's collapse.

Moving forward, she darted toward some of the smaller containers that were mostly untouched and began hauling them out of the room. It was dangerous, especially since the rest of the ceiling could cave in at any time, but without supplies, the days after the storm would be even worse. Ignoring the pain in her hand, she worked with the three men as they tried to save what they could.

Niko returned a few minutes later with pieces of scrap metal to help close off the door. He stacked it by the door and then went to help them finish gathering supplies. Daryl continued calling out instructions, but he worked alongside of them.

Skye darted back into Daryl's office for another round, but a loud *crack* made her freeze. Her gaze flew upward to the ceiling, noting the pockets of pooling water that were threatening to overflow.

Leo grabbed her arm, hauling her backward and out of the room. He shouted a warning, and the three men rushed toward the exit just as more of the ceiling crashed to the ground. Part of a beam fell, its heavy weight smacking into Niko and knocking him to the ground. His scream pierced the air.

"Niko!" Skye shouted, moving forward and dropping to the ground beside him. The beam trapped his legs, but at least it hadn't crushed his torso. There was still hope, but the longer he remained where he was, the worse his prognosis would be. She propped up his head to keep the flooding water away from his face.

Running her hand over his forehead, she said, "We're going to get you out of here. Just stay with me, Niko."

"Grab that end!" Leo shouted to Daryl and Chance, gesturing toward the opposite end of the beam.

"It's no use. It's too heavy," Chance said, grunting out the words. "Do we have any rope?"

"In one of these fucking crates," Daryl snapped. "Where's the cabling device you used earlier? We can try to rig up something to pull it off of him."

Skye frowned. They didn't have time to set up something like that. She scanned the area for something they could use as a lever. Motioning toward the corner where another smaller support beam had fallen, she shouted, "Get that beam! We can slide it under and lift it enough to pull Niko out."

Leo scrambled over the debris and grabbed the smaller

support. While the men worked together to push it under the fallen beam, Daryl grabbed one of the containers and slid it into place to use as a fulcrum.

Alanza came rushing back with Veridian in tow. They each carried sandbags in their arms.

"I heard the noise..." Alanza's voice trailed off as she spotted Niko. The sandbags fell to the ground. "Niko! No!"

"Alanza," Daryl called out, nodding his head toward Niko. "We need your help to pull him out once we lift the beam."

Alanza rushed toward them and dropped to the ground beside Niko. She grabbed his hand. "You've got this, Niko. You're gonna be just fine."

Skye noticed Veridian moving closer, and she motioned for him to stop. The water was getting higher, and it wouldn't take much to knock him over. His face paled and his eyes widened with fear. He needed a distraction, but she wasn't willing to risk him leaving her sight.

"Start stacking those sandbags by the door, V," she ordered. "Stay outside when you're finished, as close to the doorway as possible. We'll be out of here soon enough."

Turning back to Niko, she saw the pain was taking its toll on him. Running her hand over his forehead again, she said, "Just breathe, Niko. You're going to get through this just fine."

"That's what they all say right before the end," he whispered, his voice laced with agony.

"You're too pretty to die," Skye teased lightly.

He barked out a laugh. "Fuck, that hurts."

Skye's smile faded, and she tried to bury her worry.

"On three," Daryl said, gripping the end of the makeshift lever with Chance and Leo.

He shouted his count, and the men moved together as one to dislodge the beam. Skye grabbed one of Niko's arms while Alanza grabbed the other and they dragged him out of the way.

The moment he was pulled clear, the men lowered the beam back to the ground. Leo and Chance grabbed hold of Niko, lifting him and carting him out of the room and down the hall. Skye scrambled up and after them, stopping only to grab Veridian.

They hastened down the corridor back into the room they used for sleeping. It was an elevated area, so water hadn't yet flooded this room. Someone had already started setting up sandbags near the entrance, just in case. They laid Niko out on his sleeping mat and began cutting off his clothing so they could assess his injuries.

"Grab an extra blanket from the stack in the corner," Skye instructed Veridian.

She knelt beside Niko. His legs were already discolored and swelling, most likely from several fractures. Blood clots might also be a problem, but they'd need to worry about that later.

Leo grabbed the med kit they'd moved into the room earlier and opened it. He opened the container of pain medication and injected it into Niko. "It'll take a few minutes to work, but it should help with the worst of the pain. We'll brace your legs once it kicks in."

Niko nodded, his jaw still clenched in pain.

Tears sprang to Alanza's eyes, and she hastily blinked them back. Taking a seat next to Niko, she took his hand in hers. "You know, if you wanted to have a couple of women hovering over you, there are better ways to get our attention."

"It worked, didn't it?" Niko managed with a weak smile, but Skye could tell the effort cost him.

Veridian handed Skye one of their older blankets, and she quickly began cutting it into long strips. Not for the first time, she wished they had some of the more advanced

OmniLab medicine. In the trading camps, they had bone molds that could easily repair broken bones within hours.

Skye met Leo's eyes and saw the same worry reflected in his gaze. This type of injury was worse than a true break. Even if Niko survived, there was no guarantee he'd be able to walk, much less scavenge, ever again.

Daryl brought over some long pieces of metal he'd found and placed them on the ground. "See if you can brace his legs with these."

Leo picked them up and began laying them parallel to Niko's legs. Skye scooted back to give him and Chance some room to work. Veridian crept toward her, and Skye pulled him closer. He was trembling. The fear, adrenaline, and lack of sleep were too much for his seven-year-old body to handle. Taking his hand, she pulled him away from where they were beginning to lay out the strips so they could bind Niko's legs. Even with the pain killer, the process would hurt.

She sat with Veridian on their bedding and motioned for him to sit beside her. He did, and she wrapped her arm around him.

"Will Niko be okay?" he whispered, cuddling against her.

Skye ran her hand over his hair. It was tempting to lie to alleviate his fears, but she wouldn't do that to him. "Niko's strong. If anyone can recover from something like that, it's him. They're going to do everything they can to help him."

Veridian looked up at her, his brown eyes reflecting his fear. So far, he hadn't cried, but the emotion in his eyes revealed he was close to breaking.

She gave him a small smile and whispered, "Why don't you get some rest, little man? We're going to have a busy day tomorrow cleaning up everything."

He swallowed and nodded, laying his head against her. When Niko's scream ripped through the air, Veridian started trembling again. Skye pulled him tighter against her and covered his ears. Humming a wordless tune, she rocked him back and forth while they worked on Niko.

It seemed to go on for an eternity. By the time they finished, Niko had passed out. It was just as well; sleep was the best thing for him to combat the pain. At some point, Veridian's eyes had also drifted shut. Skye stroked his hair, watching as he breathed the deep and regular breaths of sleep.

Leo crouched down beside her. "Hey. Is he okay?"

She looked up to see his eyes full of concern and nodded. "Yeah. We need to get the rest of the supplies out of Daryl's office before the sun comes up, but I don't want to leave V."

Leo glanced over at Alanza who was still sitting next to Niko. It was unlikely she'd be willing to leave his side for as long as he was sleeping. They'd joined Daryl's camp around the same time as Skye, and Alanza was frequently partnered with Niko as his scavenging partner. The two of them had formed a close bond over the years, at least as close as Skye and Leo.

In a low voice, Leo asked, "Hey, Alanza? You mind keeping an eye on Veridian while Skye helps me?"

Alanza nodded. "Yeah. Someone needs to watch Niko. I'll sit with both of them."

Skye disentangled herself from Veridian, resting her hand gently on his back to make sure he didn't awaken. When he didn't move, she stood and brushed her hands on her pants, wincing at the sharp stab of pain through her hand. She hadn't had a chance to check the injury.

Leo bent down and scooped up one of the portable lights before leading her out of the sleeping area. He stopped before they got too close to Daryl's office and turned down an adjacent hall.

She arched her brow. "Where are we going? We need to get those supplies."

Leo didn't answer right away. He led her into one of the abandoned rooms of the building. "We're going to need to convert this room into Daryl's new office."

Skye swept her gaze over the room. It was the same as any other, except full of debris. They could push most of it to the side for the time being to create a usable space for Daryl and some of their storage items.

She brushed her hair away from her face. "You want to do this now? Or just move the supplies in here?"

Leo turned toward her and put the light on the ground beside them. Gesturing to her hand, he said, "I want to know how you're feeling."

She frowned. "It hurts, but I'm glad I didn't use the last of the pain medication. Niko's going to be in for a rough time when it wears off." She lifted her injured hand and wrinkled her nose. "This is nothing compared to that."

"There's a good chance Niko won't make it," Leo admitted quietly. "I've seen injuries like his before. If we can't get additional medical supplies from OmniLab, we may have to end his suffering. I don't think any of us want to watch him slowly die in pain."

Skye squeezed her eyes shut. She'd seen injuries like his too. The potential for complications and not healing properly was enormous. None of them could make that decision for Niko though. "I need to take Veridian out of camp if it comes to that. He won't understand."

Leo cupped her cheek with his hand, and she immediately leaned into his touch. He ran his thumb across her cheek and whispered, "If I hadn't stopped you from going back into Daryl's office..." He paused. "I don't want to think about what could have happened."

Opening her eyes, she saw the raw pain in his expression. Realizing his need for reassurance was as great as hers, Skye took a step closer to him and placed her hands against his chest. Leo's heart beat steadily beneath her fingertips, and she swallowed. It could have just as easily been him.

"You were standing right where Niko was just seconds earlier." The thought made her feel lightheaded, and she gripped his shirt tighter. A lump formed in her throat, and she hastily blinked back the tears threatening to escape. "I can't lose you, Leo."

"Baby," he whispered, searching her expression, "if you need to cry, go ahead."

She nodded, understanding immediately why Leo had brought her in here. It would be hard enough for Veridian to cope without witnessing his mother falling apart too.

Skye let the tears fall, and Leo pulled her close, burying his face in her hair. Leaning against him, she wrapped her arms around him and listened to the reassuring sound of his heart beating. Leo held her for a long time, rubbing his hand up and down her back. They stayed like that for a long time, silently conveying everything that mattered. They were both alive, and with any luck, they'd continue to remain that way.

Taking a steadying breath, Skye forced herself to push aside her fears and focus on what needed to be done. The longer they stayed in here, the less time they had to move their supplies before more were ruined by the storm. Lifting her head to look up into Leo's eyes, she said, "Thank you."

He gave her a small smile and cupped her cheek. "You don't ever have to thank me."

"I do," she said, running her hands over his chest again. "You always seem to know what I need."

"It's no more than what you'd do for me, Skye."

She nodded, lowering her gaze to study his shirt. It was damp under her fingertips, both from the rain and his exertion. "When the sun comes up, we can power up the med scanner to find out the extent of the damage to Niko's legs. The pain medication won't last more than six hours though."

Leo was silent for a long time. He trailed the back of his fingers down her cheek, and she knew he was thinking and weighing all the possibilities in his mind. "There's one more dose of pain medication before we're completely out. We can give him a blood thinner too. We have a few things we can trade for additional medical supplies, but not enough."

She frowned. "We still have a bunch of people in the ruins. Maybe they were able to scavenge some items before the storm hit."

"We'll hope, but we can't count on it," Leo said quietly, his expression turning grim. "If you're ready, let's go see what we can salvage from Daryl's office. As soon as the storm lets up, we'll have a better idea about what we have to trade."

Skye nodded, and he picked up the portable light. It was going to be a long night, and even longer until the storm finally abated. But as long as Leo was by her side, they'd get through it together.

CHAPTER FOUR

LEO GLANCED down at the crate he was inventorying, comparing the contents with the information on his tablet. Despite their efforts, the majority of their excess supplies had been destroyed. They'd managed to salvage some items, but there were fewer remaining supplies than expected.

It had been two days since Skye had almost fallen off the roof and Niko had been injured. Some of their people were still holed up in the ruins. The worst of the storm had finally passed earlier that morning. Once it was safe enough to travel, their people would be heading back. The scavenging teams had a few emergency rations with them, but only enough for a day or two. With any luck, they'd just be tired and hungry, but there was no way to know until they arrived.

Hopefully, Skye's actions on the roof had prevented severe injuries. They'd been fortunate enough to get out an emergency signal, but it hadn't done her any good. She was still favoring her hand a little too much. The longer Skye's hand took to heal, the more likely the wound sealer would fail and increase the chances of infection.

Leo would continue to watch it, but he needed to

consider some other options before it got to that point. That didn't even take into account the medical supplies Niko needed to recover from his injuries. His agonizing cries could be heard throughout the camp when he was not unconscious. If they didn't get more medical supplies soon, it was unlikely Niko would survive the week.

Trying to keep Veridian away from Niko, Skye instructed Veridian on how to purify the water they'd been collecting from the storm. At least they didn't have to worry about water for a while, even if nothing else good had come from the heavy rains. Skye and Veridian worked together to ladle purified water into hydrating packs and then sealed them. It was simple enough work and Veridian was eager to help his mother.

Leo sighed and tried to ignore his growing headache. One good score in the ruins would remove a lot of pressure. They needed to get back to scavenging as soon as possible.

Skye laughed at something Veridian said, and Leo lifted his head to observe the two of them. Her blue eyes twinkled in the artificial light of the workroom, and he couldn't help but smile in response. Skye lit up the entire room when she laughed, and it brought some light into all their lives. Everyone within the camp had been charmed by her on some level, and she added some much-needed levity to their existence.

As though sensing his gaze on her, she glanced over at him and her eyes warmed. The sight was enough to make him debate whether or not to put aside the inventory and join them. It was difficult keeping his distance from her, but it was necessary to keep camp gossip to a minimum. Everyone knew he was sleeping with her, but as the camp leader's second-in-command, perceptions of favoritism could easily work against Skye. Leo wasn't willing to risk it.

Daryl already had reservations about Skye's continued

worth to their camp given her son had come with her. Most people with children lived in family camps in some of the outlying areas. Skye had managed to buy a position when she was pregnant with Veridian, but after so many years, Daryl's goodwill had disappeared. Despite their best efforts to scavenge enough artifacts to trade, Veridian was still another mouth to feed and their resources were few. It would be better once the boy was older and able to contribute more, but that would take time.

Skye brushed her blond hair away from her face, her smile fading at the sight of someone standing behind him. Leo tensed, knowing it was one of a handful of people who would make those charming dimples of hers disappear.

"Leo," Daryl said. "I need a word with you."

Leo held Skye's gaze for a moment before she turned away to help Veridian fill another hydrating pack. With a sigh, Leo put his tablet on the top of the supply crate. He followed their camp leader down the corridor and into the room they'd temporarily set up as an office. It was private, which didn't bode well.

Daryl turned to face him, his expression grim. He was only a dozen years Leo's senior, but the deep lines on his face made him appear a great deal older. "Niko's not doing any better. Alanza doesn't think he's going to pull through."

Leo nodded. "She told me this morning. We used the last of our pain medication on him yesterday. He's got multiple compound fractures. If we can't get a bone mold to correct it, he won't heal properly."

"We don't have enough in tradable goods to afford that," Daryl said with a sigh. "I've also got some concerns about Skye. When she doesn't think anyone's watching, it's obvious her hand pains her. She could barely grip a screwdriver earlier. Chance said it's pretty bad, but she brushes it off when he's asked. Has she told you anything?"

Dammit.

Leo tried to keep his expression neutral. He'd been expecting this discussion but had hoped she'd be doing a bit better by now. The metabolic booster must have lost its effectiveness. Sometimes, the OmniLab traders gave them older equipment that was at the end of its life expectancy.

It wouldn't help Skye or Veridian if he handled Daryl's inquiry poorly. Daryl wasn't an evil man, but based on Leo's initial inventory of the camp's dwindling supplies, their situation was becoming dire. They'd likely have to make some difficult decisions soon. With Niko and Skye injured, that meant both their positions within the camp were in jeopardy.

"Skye took a huge risk on that roof, Daryl. We managed to get a warning out to everyone about the storm so they could find shelter. Thanks to her, we still have an operating camp."

Daryl crossed his arms over his chest. "You didn't answer my question. How much damage did she do?"

Leo sighed. "It's a deep wound, but she still has mobility in her fingers. We won't know more for a while."

Daryl rubbed his temples as though trying to ward off a headache. "You know I like her, Leo. That's not what this is about. Hell, if I could pick and choose people to stay based on personal preference, it wouldn't be an issue. She's a good worker and always willing to do whatever is necessary to get shit done. But if she can't work, I can't keep her and Veridian here."

Trying to keep his temper in check, Leo didn't respond right away. If Daryl kept pushing him on this, they were going to have a serious problem between them. "What are you suggesting? We toss her and the kid out because she got hurt trying to save our people? Fuck that, Daryl. You want a mutiny on your hands? Keep walking down that path."

Daryl frowned, anger flaring briefly in his eyes. "Don't

threaten me, Leo. We're likely going to lose Niko, and he's a damn good scavenger. I need people who can work. If Skye's injury takes weeks or months to heal, we can't afford to support her and Veridian for all that time. She can come back eventually if she wants, but you need to be objective about her. *This* is why I don't tolerate emotional shit in my camp."

Leo stiffened. "I'm keeping an eye on the injury. But keep in mind, we don't know what shape our people will be in when they return. If any of them are hurt too badly, you're going to need Skye to help get things done. In the meantime, she'll work. That woman will sacrifice anything and everything to keep this camp functional. Even with her injury, she's been hauling crates and working right alongside the rest of us. I've scheduled her to go back into the ruins tomorrow. I'll be with her."

The camp leader nodded, his shoulders relaxing slightly. "All right. We'll give it a few more days. But if she can't produce…" His voice trailed off, and he sighed. "I know what I'm asking isn't easy, Leo, but you're my second-in-command for a reason. I need you to try to put aside your feelings for her and consider what's in the best interest of our camp."

Leo's jaw clenched, but he inclined his head.

Daryl walked over to the crate he'd been using as a makeshift desk and picked up a tablet. "This last storm was one of the worst I've ever seen. If this was an indicator about what the rest of the season has in store for us, we're in serious trouble. We have at least another month of these storms and only two or three more days of supplies left. When you're finished with the inventory, let me know. We're going to need to run an assessment of everyone's productivity scores. We may not have a choice about making some hard decisions."

Leo gave him a curt nod. "I'll do what needs to be done."

Without saying another word, Leo turned and left the room. He managed to keep his temper under control, but just barely. He'd meant what he said about doing what needed to be done—he'd do whatever the hell was necessary to keep Skye there. Those family camps weren't safe for someone like her or for a kid like Veridian. He didn't want to think about what could happen to them in a place like that. Skye was beautiful and too damn sweet for her own good. And Veridian... hell, the boy had a sensitive soul. Neither one of them were suited to that sort of life. Going back there might destroy the precious spark inside both of them.

Leo clenched his fists in frustration. If Skye hadn't been so protective of their campmates, she wouldn't be in this position now. It had been an easy enough assignment: get on the roof, check the equipment, and get the hell off. But she always cared too much about everyone, even to the point she'd sacrifice herself for them. It was noble, but they couldn't afford nobility. He needed her to stay safe. Or as safe as possible, given the precariousness of their lives.

Heading back into the workroom, Leo approached Skye and Veridian. She lifted her head, searching his expression, and frowned. Brushing her uninjured hand over Veridian's hair, she said, "V, why don't you keep working here? I need to talk to Leo. Just make sure to test the contamination levels on each hydrating pack before you seal them. If any of them aren't within the parameters I showed you, put them off to the side for me."

Veridian looked up at Leo with brown eyes that were far too perceptive. "Daryl's mad again, isn't he? Is he going to make us leave?"

Before Leo could respond, Skye crouched down beside Veridian and tilted his chin to meet his eyes. "Does it matter where we are?"

Veridian frowned. "I don't want to go."

"Location isn't important, V," she reminded him, her voice gentle. She traced a heart over his chest and added,

"What matters are the people we care about. We're survivors, and we'll do whatever is necessary to keep surviving. Remember that."

When Veridian nodded, Skye smiled. "Good. Now, how about you finish working on these hydrating packs for me? I'll be back in a few minutes."

"Okay."

"Thanks, little man." She kissed his cheek before standing.

Leo frowned. Sometimes, he worried Skye protected the boy too much. Veridian would eventually need a bit of hardening if he was going to survive what life handed him in the future. Unfortunately, those lessons would likely come sooner than any of them hoped.

Not trusting himself to speak before he got Skye alone, Leo led her back into the empty room where they slept. Rudimentary sleeping mats had been sandwiched together on the floor. He usually slept beside her and Veridian, and Skye frequently curled up against him at night. Holding her and listening to the soft sounds of her breathing while he fell asleep was more peaceful than anything he'd ever experienced. The sight of their sleeping mats beside one another only reinforced his need to do whatever was necessary to keep her with him.

Leo turned back around to look into Skye's worried eyes, wanting to reassure her but knowing he needed to be honest.

"Well, damn," she murmured, taking a step toward him. "Your expression is about as unpleasant as that storm. How bad is it? Was Veridian right? Does Daryl want us to leave?"

Leo sighed and shook his head. "Not yet. Our supply levels are lower than we expected. Daryl's concerned about Niko and your hand. Chance was running his mouth again and told him your injury was bad."

Skye gave him a small smile. "Did you expect any different? Chance is the best source of gossip this side of the Omni Towers."

He blew out a breath. "Yeah, and I intend to have words with him about keeping his mouth shut. He doesn't need to be causing more problems around here. Daryl's about to snap. I think we all are."

She tilted her head and took a step closer to him. "You can't give Chance too hard of a time. It's been tough around here the past few days. We're all going a bit stir-crazy wondering what's happening with everyone still in the ruins, but it'll get better soon enough. Now, how bad is the situation with Daryl?"

"I'll take care of Daryl. I don't want you to worry about it," Leo said, realizing he was trying to reassure her just like she'd done with Veridian.

Skye frowned, her eyes becoming suspicious. "You'd better not be thinking about putting your position in jeopardy by covering for me, Leo. The risk on that roof was mine to take. I want your word that you won't sacrifice your future for me."

"No," he said, refusing to make any such promise. As far as he was concerned, *she* was his future. At least, the only future he wanted. "I told Daryl you were going back into the ruins with me tomorrow."

Skye blinked up at him with those gorgeous blue eyes of hers. "Not that I'm objecting to some alone time with you, but even if we go to the ruins, some of those areas are going to be flooded or weakened. We'll need to take extra supplies with us just in case, but the camp only has enough food for another few days." She frowned and shook her head. "This storm messed up everything. We haven't managed to scavenge anything in the past three days."

Unable to resist touching her, Leo reached over to take her uninjured hand in his and his ran his thumb over the back of it. "I need you to trust me, baby. I have a plan. There's a spot I discovered that should prove to be profitable."

Skye arched an eyebrow and gave him a teasing smile. "A new spot? Just the two of us? I'm starting to wish that metabolic booster had worked a bit better. You might have to settle for just one of my hands on you."

He chuckled. No one else had ever been able to coax him out of his darkest moods, except for her. "Are you trying to distract me?"

Her smile deepened. "Is it working?"

Skye had no idea just how much she affected him. His gaze roamed over her face and then downward over her soft curves. He barely resisted the urge to groan. If he had his way, he'd spend the next several hours getting lost in her. Even having her this close was a special kind of torment. "If you were any more distracting, I'd never get any work done."

She bit her lip, drawing his attention back to her mouth. The urge to kiss her was nearly overpowering. Trailing her hand over his chest, she urged, "Tell me more about this secret spot you've found."

Leo moved even closer to her so he was just inches away. He wasn't willing to tell anyone else what he'd discovered yet. They needed every advantage, even with their own campmates. The only reason he hadn't told Skye was because she worried when he went to dangerous areas alone.

"I started mapping the area a few weeks ago when you were scavenging with Chance in Sector Three. This area's a higher-risk zone, but I think we should try it."

Skye tilted her head, giving him another teasing smile. "Excitement? A little danger? You always know how to show a girl a good time."

"And I intend to keep doing it," Leo said with a grin. "Can you make sure Alanza will keep an eye on Veridian for you tomorrow? We'll be gone most of the day."

She nodded. "Yeah. Alanza won't want to leave Niko anytime soon. She won't have a problem watching Veridian. I'll give him a few projects to keep him busy, just in case Niko's condition worsens."

He squeezed her hand and released her as Chance walked into the room.

Chance glanced over at them. "Yo, Skye, your kid's trying to teach Daryl how to purify water. You might want to make sure he doesn't get dunked."

Skye muttered a curse and hastened out of the room to run interference. Leo chuckled. Veridian was a cute kid, but Daryl didn't have much patience.

Leo ran a hand over his closely cropped hair and considered his plan. Hopefully, if things worked out tomorrow, they'd be able to get the medical supplies they needed to help Niko *and* secure Skye's position within the camp. Otherwise, he'd need to consider a more drastic solution. He wasn't willing to lose Skye or Veridian. The kid had managed to work his way into his heart, right alongside his mother.

CHAPTER FIVE

SKYE BENT down to finish checking the solar collectors on Leo's speeder. A few of them were starting to get run down, but they were still functional. Sometimes, that was the best they could hope for. She lifted her head, staring again in the direction of the Omni Towers. Her life had been drastically different just a few short years ago, but OmniLab had changed everything. Even so, she couldn't regret the past. It had given her one of the best things in her life.

"You about ready?"

Skye stood at the sound of Leo's voice and nodded, shoving her multipurpose tool back into her jacket pocket. "Yeah. Your speeder's going to need a few adjustments soon, but we'll be good for today. You should probably run a full diagnostic on it soon."

Leo walked toward her and attached the cabling device to his vehicle. "I'm thinking about going to the towers again and banging on their damn doors. If we can't find anything to scavenge today, that's going to be my next stop. We need those medical supplies, and I'm not going to take no for an answer. At the very least, you need another metabolic booster and some antibiotics."

She darted a quick glance at him and frowned. Last night, he'd been quieter than usual. Not even her usual teasing had managed to pull him out of his dark mood.

A few of their people had come back late yesterday. Riven had a broken arm and Pepper had a sprained ankle, which would prevent both of them from scavenging for a while. They were still waiting on word from the rest of their crew. The longer they went without returning, the more likely they had serious injuries.

Unfortunately, it was growing increasingly likely that Daryl would ask Skye to leave. With so many people unable to work, it only made sense to cut loose those who were the biggest drain on their limited resources. The fact she was supporting Veridian placed her at the forefront of the chopping block. She faced the same uncertainty every month. It was only a matter of time before Daryl forced her out. If she was honest with herself, she'd been lucky to have lasted this long. The only thing that had likely saved her so far was Leo's interference, but he'd never admit to it.

Skye finished packing the bag of supplies into the speeder carrying case. "I appreciate the thought, but going to the towers won't do much good. If OmniLab wouldn't help me a year ago when Veridian got sick, they won't help us now. Our best option is still to trade for supplies with one of the trading camps."

Leo's jaw clenched, and he picked up his helmet. "The whole thing pisses me off. Did they at least give the asshole the message when you went to the towers?"

Skye shrugged. "I don't think they believed me. Why would they? I'm just another ruin rat."

"This is just one more reason those traders are worthless cocksuckers. He lied to you, Skye. He knew what life was like here, and he stayed just long enough to get you pregnant. Now he's back in those towers enjoying who knows what comforts while you and his son are down here."

Skye shook her head. Leo's anger made sense, at least on the surface, but he hadn't known Tyler or the type of man he'd been. Tyler *had* cared. She couldn't fault him for leaving her. He'd made his position clear before they'd ever gotten involved. What happened between them had been her choice.

Running her gloved fingers over her well-worn helmet, she said, "You're too hard on him, Leo. It was at the end of Tyler's trading commission. He hadn't been back to the towers in a couple of years. His birth control implant must have failed early. I didn't realize I was pregnant until after he left. It wouldn't have changed anything, but he didn't know."

"The rest of his camp knew you were sleeping with him," Leo argued, checking the controls on his UV guard with a bit more force than was necessary. This had always been a sensitive subject between them, and she usually avoided it for exactly that reason. For Leo to be bringing it up now meant he was looking for a fight. Either that or he was looking for someone to blame for his current frustrations, and OmniLab was a convenient target.

Leo glanced over at her and scowled. "The new trader should have sent word to him. It's just one more indication they don't give a shit about any of us. They at least should have given you a way to collect supplies or something."

Skye shrugged, unable to dispute Leo's words. She'd thought them often enough over the years, but holding on to her anger didn't change anything.

When she'd realized she was pregnant, Skye *had* gone to the new trader. He was pompous and arrogant, refusing to believe her claims about Tyler being the father of her unborn child. As he put it, "no one from the towers would sully themselves enough to sleep with a ruin rat." It was just one more slap in the face. Even though she'd worked alongside the trading camp crew for almost two years, it had been made clear that her life was inconsequential compared to those who lived within the towers. It didn't matter that Veridian shared part of that birthright.

Skye blew out a breath, trying to release the anger the memory evoked. Leo was right; most of the traders didn't care much about them either way. The new trader probably *did* believe her—he simply hadn't cared.

Instead, he'd terminated her contract with the trading camp prematurely. She'd been fortunate enough to receive a severance package and had used all of it to buy a place within Daryl's camp for herself and Veridian. But all contracts had an expiration date, and she'd already exceeded hers.

Leo unobtrusively helped out quite a bit, but trying to earn enough credits to retain her place and Veridian's was growing increasingly challenging. Not only did Skye need to keep both of them fed and healthy, but they also required special clothing and gear so they could traverse the surface. It would be less expensive to live in one of the family camps, but much more dangerous. She didn't want that life for Veridian.

"It doesn't matter. If Veridian had gone to the towers, I wouldn't have been able to see him grow up. At least this way, I get to have him in my life." She lifted her head to stare into the distance. The towers were too far away to be seen from here, but the glimpse she'd gotten from the roof had been burned into her memory. "It sucks to say it, but I'd give Veridian up in a second if I knew he'd have a better life there. Sometimes, I worry I won't be around to protect him as he grows up."

"Hey," Leo placed his hand over hers, "you will be. I'll

make sure of it. And I'll protect him too. You and Veridian will be fine."

Skye swallowed and nodded, acknowledging Leo's promise. She wouldn't regret the time she spent with Tyler because of the precious gift she'd received in Veridian. And that decision had ultimately led her to Leo.

Unlike Tyler, Leo understood her. They shared a common background the former OmniLab trader had never been able to truly comprehend. Tyler had been a brief fling, but Leo was the one who had truly captured her heart. His gruff exterior was nothing more than a ruse to keep people at a distance. It had intrigued her enough to want to chisel away at the façade, and what she'd found below the surface was more rewarding than anything she ever thought possible.

Skye turned her hand upside down, interlacing her fingers with his. "Maybe I'll be the one to protect you instead. I kinda like having you around. You're awfully nice to look at."

Leo's eyes warmed, and he squeezed her hand. "Come on, baby. Let's get going. We have a long drive ahead of us."

She nodded and climbed on the back of his speeder. Wrapping her arms around his waist, she held on as he pulled out of their camp.

———

THE DRIVE to the ruins was hot and miserable. Skye's UV jacket stuck to her skin while her hair was plastered to her head under her helmet. This time of year was always bad, with the weather alternating between scorching heat and furious storms. They rarely knew which to expect, and the sudden fluctuations required them to be ready to seek shelter at a moment's notice. Unfortunately, it also had the unwanted effect of burning up some of their equipment faster than necessary.

Skye studied the crumbling ruins and abandoned streets, somewhat surprised by the direction Leo had taken them. They'd traveled closer to OmniLab and the southeast trading district, where a large portion of the ground had shifted and formed a deep chasm more than a century earlier. She didn't know what had caused it, but many of the ruined buildings within the area had fallen into it.

Her skin prickled as a strange awareness filled her, and she frowned. The entire area felt eerie. She wouldn't have considered coming here on her own, and even now, her instincts were warning her about some unknown danger. Maybe she was overreacting, but she didn't believe that. Skye had never scared easily. Even when she'd worked in Tyler's trading camp, their crew had been reluctant to scavenge there. Strange accidents seemed to occur whenever people went too deep underground. Most people were perfectly content to avoid this entire area, herself included.

Leo turned the speeder more to the north, and her arms tightened reflexively around his waist as they drove even closer. This was more than risky, but she trusted him. Leo never would have brought her here if the situation wasn't dire. She didn't want to think about what would befall Veridian if anything happened to them, but the alternative of not being able to provide critical supplies for their camp was equally as bad.

Leo pulled into an abandoned building right on the outside of the chasm. Skye climbed off the vehicle and waited while he secured it. The building wasn't much to look at, more of a hollowed-out shell than anything. It had once been some type of commercial outpost, maybe a small store. Broken shelving units lined the deteriorated walls of the building, but the contents had long since been cleared out. The shelving units could be salvaged for parts, but there was no point in bothering with them. Their camp moved around too frequently for them to be able to utilize more permanent fixtures.

Leo motioned for Skye to follow him, and she grabbed the bag of supplies she'd brought with her while he picked up another larger bag. They'd normally leave them with the speeder, but the chasm prevented them from getting too close to the ruins where they were planning to scavenge. If they had more time and reliable equipment, they could have approached from another direction, but neither was a luxury they could afford.

They hiked a short distance until they approached an even larger building right on the edge of the chasm. Judging by what was left and the amount of rubble, it had once stood several stories high. The building was large enough that dozens of families could have lived in it before they decided to abandon it.

Climbing over a pile of debris, Skye entered the apartment building through a missing window. The glass had disappeared some years before, most likely broken and then later ground into dust. Adjusting the light on her helmet to account for the darkness, she swept her gaze over the area as Leo led her deeper into the building. They tested each step carefully before moving forward, their boots crunching over the debris. This building didn't appear to have suffered any flooding from the storm, but wind damage and time had taken its toll.

Their footsteps were the only sound in the eerie stillness, giving Skye the impression they were the only two people left alive in the world. It was difficult to imagine this place had once been teeming with life. But now, it was as though nature had decided to reclaim this entire area. Year after year, the man-made structures surrendered to the inevitable, just as many of the human residents had done.

A narrow and partially collapsed staircase led downward

into what once was some sort of underground parking area. Skye continued to follow Leo, guessing they were heading toward another entrance to the chasm.

Leo stopped in one of the lower levels of the underground parking garage. The remains of a few ancient automobiles were still present, but age had rendered them mostly useless. They might be able to pick apart some of the components to use in their camp, but that would require more manpower than just the two of them. Once they got a better handle on what supplies they needed, they could arrange to bring more people back here to collect additional parts.

Leo removed his helmet and Skye did the same, disengaging the audio of her commlink system to conserve power. Although she could talk back and forth with Leo, they'd traveled too far outside their camp's limited communication range to be able to reach them.

She scanned the parking area. It was surprisingly untouched, considering its location. "You always bring me to the nicest places."

He chuckled. "I did some exploring a few weeks ago and discovered this garage connects with another building. We should be able to cross into it and see what we can find over there."

Tucking her helmet under her arm, she adjusted the heavy bag over her shoulder. "How far did you explore?"

Leo frowned, his gaze sweeping the garage. "Only far enough to realize it leads directly into the buildings within the chasm. We're firmly within OmniLab territory, and those traders won't take kindly to us scavenging here. We should be able to keep our presence masked if they're anywhere on the surface. I think we're too far underground for them to pick up anything."

Skye nodded. "Where's the entrance?"

"Just up ahead." Leo gestured to the opposite end of the

garage. "We'll leave most of our gear here. Once we pass through, we'll need mobility more than anything. Leave your helmet too. We can't risk using the communication equipment and alerting OmniLab to our frequencies."

Skye placed her belongings on the ground, opening the bag to pull out a small carrying pack. She put only the essentials inside, which consisted of a few tools, hydrating packs, and a couple of nutrient bars. She'd intentionally left enough space to store any items they discovered. Glancing over at Leo, she saw he was doing the same with his bag. When they both finished, she walked with Leo down the sloping floor even deeper underground.

"It's cooler down here," she said, keeping her voice quiet. Sound tended to carry in some of these buildings, and the effect could be somewhat disorienting.

"Yeah," he murmured, moving in front of her to lead the way. "I've thought about talking to Daryl about moving our camp into one of these garages. It might help to conserve some of our equipment, but it's a little close to OmniLab."

"I'm surprised it hasn't flooded," Skye admitted, ducking under a partially collapsed column.

"Yeah. There are a lot of weird things about this whole area. I've never been able to figure out how everything's in ruins, but the Omni Towers have remained standing for centuries. Something's a little strange about them. Even this chasm stops before it gets anywhere near the towers."

She made a small noise of agreement. "I asked Tyler about that once."

Leo glanced back at her. "Did he tell you?"

Skye shook her head. "No. He said something about a circle, but he wouldn't elaborate."

"A circle? Like their emblem?" Leo pointed out an area where the floor was depressed. Such a dip was usually an indication of weakness in the structural members. If they stepped there, it might cause the floor to collapse or worse. It was best to avoid those areas whenever possible.

"Hell if I know," she muttered, making sure to keep her steps following Leo's exact path. "I thought their emblem was an 'O' for OmniLab, but Tyler said there was more to it. He called it an 'ouroboros' or something. It's a snake biting its tail."

"That's fitting," Leo said, gesturing toward another place that looked weaker, indicating she should avoid it. "They're all snakes as far as I'm concerned. Did he say anything else?"

"Bits and pieces. Tyler wasn't exactly forthcoming with information, and I wasn't eager to jeopardize my paycheck by asking too many questions. I got the impression he was uneasy about saying too much—maybe even afraid."

Leo glanced back at her and frowned. "Afraid of what? Not being allowed back in the towers?"

"I don't think so," Skye said quietly, somewhat surprised by Leo's curiosity. He didn't usually ask about her time with the trading camp, preferring to leave the past where it belonged. "I once overheard a commlink call he was having with someone back in the towers—his sister, I think. She was involved with someone important in the towers, and Tyler freaked out about it. He started yelling about a circle and that she was jeopardizing everything."

"The circle again?"

"Yeah." She ducked under a beam that had partially fallen. "He acted strange after that call. He started talking about staying on the surface and even bringing his sister to live here. He asked me a lot of questions about what life had been like growing up here."

Leo glanced back at her again. "No shit?"

Skye shrugged. "He never said anything more after that night. I guess my description of life here was worse than whatever had him freaked about the towers. It was only a month later that he left to go back."

"Hmm," Leo murmured and then fell silent, testing the floor in front of him. "We're getting close. The next building is just up a little farther."

She glanced around him. A doorway was ahead of them, and the garage angled toward it. "How far did you go?"

"Only far enough to take a quick look. I didn't have an opportunity to explore. Besides, I knew you'd want to come down here."

She couldn't help but smile. "Aw, Leo, I'm touched. You wanted to share all the good loot with me?"

He chuckled, motioning for her to walk in front of him. "Yeah, well, let's see what we find in here first. If this building is mostly intact, we should get a good haul."

She grinned and moved forward. A staircase went up into the next building. It was in better condition than the one they'd just left, which was promising. A few of the stairs were broken, but they should be able to climb up easily.

"A high-risk area? Valuable artifacts just waiting for my little hands? You're getting me all hot and bothered, Leo. I'm surprised you waited so long to bring me here."

Leo snorted and swatted her butt. "Move your ass, Skye. We've got work to do."

Pressing her hand against the wall, she tested it for soundness. When it didn't give way or collapse, she started to climb. They'd probably work through the first level of the building and then move upward. If this was an apartment building, the most valuable items would probably be found in the individual living units. Unfortunately, the closer they got to the surface, the more likely the floors would have already been picked clean. Their best bet would be to check the lower levels first.

Skye finished climbing the first flight of stairs, stepping

carefully through to what appeared to be a common area for the building. Ancient furnishings, some crumbling with the passage of time, were all covered by a heavy blanket of dust. She walked over to what appeared to be an expansive desk and began trying to pry open the cabinets. Leo started poking around on the other side of the room, picking up different items and pocketing others.

The cabinet creaked and groaned open, and the door hinges broke apart at the intrusion. She placed the cabinet door on the floor and began digging through the contents. It was mostly papers, and they started to crumble the moment she began rifling through them. She found a handful of old-fashioned coins, but they were novelties, nothing more.

Whenever their scavenging camp needed items, they sometimes tried to barter or trade between other ruin rat camps. It was only with the OmniLab traders that they were extended lines of credit to purchase certain critical goods and supplies. Medicine, technical equipment, and some foodstuffs were hard to come by among the surface camps. In her experience, OmniLab always had the best toys.

Skye scooped up the coins and dropped them into her pouch. During her time working in the trading camp, she'd learned quite a bit about the types of items OmniLab was most interested in acquiring. They didn't care much for the precious metals or equipment the ruin rat camps prized. Instead, they were interested in trinkets or decorative items. Most of these things had cultural or historical significance, but they did little as far as helping anyone to survive.

The lessons she'd learned in Tyler's trading camp had come in handy. Skye had shared that knowledge with Leo, and they'd both found their scavenging hauls had become much more profitable. She'd also started schooling Veridian on the history of the area, bringing him old video files, books, or other items she discovered. If Veridian could learn more about what items might be interesting to the Omnis, it would only help him survive later. He'd proven to be an apt pupil, eager to study anything and everything related to pre-war cultures.

Skye pulled open a drawer and it came apart in her hand. Ducking down, she reached into the crevice to unceremoniously scoop out the contents. A small chain fell out, tiny enough it would fit around her wrist. It must have been overlooked or fallen behind the drawer centuries earlier.

"Find something?" Leo moved to stand beside her.

"Looks like a bracelet," she said, standing up to study it. It was mostly metal, but there was a small green stone in the center. "It's nothing remarkable, but it'll be worth at least a few hundred credits. Maybe more if it cleans up well. Those Omnis like their sparklies."

Leo nodded, scanning the room again. "I don't think we're going to find much in here. I'm starting to think these aren't residences at all, but rather some sort of big commercial area. It's all indoors. There's an exit right over there. I looked, and there are some other places that probably have a ton of loot. There must be dozens of stores out there."

Skye dropped the bracelet into her bag and rubbed her injured hand. "If we can manage to find a few thousand credits' worth of artifacts, it'll take some of the pressure off. We can come back in a few days for a better haul."

"Your hand's bothering you again, isn't it?"

She glanced over at Leo to find him frowning. He always worried too much. She offered him a smile. "It's fine. Just a few twinges."

Leo walked over to her and captured her hand in his. He turned it over so her palm was facing upward, but it was too heavily bandaged to see anything.

"A few twinges, my ass. I told you to tell me if it was getting worse. If it's bothering you this much, chances are good an infection's setting in. You tried to do too much with moving supplies around during that storm."

"Leo," she began, starting to withdraw her hand but he held it tightly. "I'm going to be fine. It's sore, but that's to be expected."

"Dammit, Skye," Leo muttered, his gaze hardening. "We're not leaving here until we find something we can trade for another metabolic booster and a round of antibiotics. I'm not willing to risk anything happening to you."

She narrowed her eyes at him. "If we earn enough for those supplies, they need to go to Niko. I'm not any more special than anyone in our camp, and this injury is nothing compared to what he's going through. You need to stop treating me differently."

Leo took a step closer, his eyes flashing dangerously. "Fuck that. You *are* special... to me. I don't give a shit about the rest of them."

"Liar," she retorted, inclining her head in challenge. "You care about every single person in our camp. You're the one always running interference with Daryl. You're the one who sneaks Veridian extra portions of our rations, especially the sweets. You're the one who adjusts people's schedules if they're not feeling well or have an injury. You cover for all of us, Leo. You *protect* all of us. And that's exactly why you're going to be the best camp leader we've ever seen—because you care."

Leo grabbed her and hauled her against him, lowering his head to take possession of her mouth. Unable to resist him or his unspoken demand, Skye wound her arms around his neck and softened her body against him. Desire, strong and heady, flowed through her, and she showed him with her kiss how much she wanted him. Down here, below the surface and away from the prying eyes of their camp, they could be free to embrace their true emotions.

When she whimpered, wanting more, Leo suddenly broke the kiss. She panted, staring up at him in surprise. Barely restrained passion filled the space between them, but he didn't kiss her again. Instead, Leo shook his head.

"Don't think you're going to distract me, baby. As much as I want you, I need you healthy more."

Her insides melted at the look in his eyes and the depth of emotion she saw within them. "I probably shouldn't enjoy trying to distract you so much, but I can't seem to help myself where you're concerned. You're always so serious at camp. I like seeing the real you."

Leo swallowed. "Skye, baby——"

She lifted her hands to cup his face. "This. Right here. This is who you are. Strong but compassionate. Determined but impassioned." She trailed her fingertips along his jaw. "Don't hide from me, Leo. You can wear a mask when we're in camp, but never with me."

"I don't know how you do it," he murmured, his gaze softening as he searched her expression. "I'm not perfect, but I feel like I can accomplish anything with you by my side. You make me want to be a better man. I never believed someone like you could exist."

Skye swallowed, the intensity in his gaze making her heart soar. No one else had ever made her feel this way. It was humbling and empowering at the same time. "You're better than you believe, Leo. I've always known who you are. I see it every day." She placed her hand over his heart. "It's one of the many reasons I fell in love with you."

"Skye, you shouldn't——"

She placed her fingertips against his lips to silence his objections. "We're not in Daryl's camp right now. I don't care what he says about emotional entanglements. Not saying the words doesn't make it any less true. I love you, Leo."

Leo rested his forehead against hers and tightened his

hands on her hips. "You're impossible to resist, Skye. I started falling for you the moment you stepped foot in Daryl's camp. You'd lost everything, but you were so damn fierce and determined. You faced me and Daryl down, demanding we give you a place in the camp."

She laughed at the description. "It seemed to work well enough. But you were far more intimidating than Daryl."

His mouth curved upward. "But you don't find me intimidating now."

"No," Skye admitted with a small smile and placed her hand over Leo's heart again. "I know what kind of man you are now. I admire you in so many ways."

His eyes softened. "You've become the most important thing in the world to me. These moments with you just aren't enough. One day, when I'm camp leader, we're going to stop hiding what's between us."

"We're free to be true to each other down here," Skye whispered, needing to show him with more than words the depth of her emotion for him. She wanted to erase all his worries, even if it was just for a short time.

"I need you, Skye," Leo murmured, wrapping his arms around her and drawing her closer. He lowered his head again, claiming her mouth. She knew he was worried about her injury and would refuse to leave until they found something, but life was fleeting. Happiness needed to be grasped whenever they could find it, and with Leo, she'd found a piece of hers.

He kissed her, but it was more than just a gentle pressure of his mouth against hers. His lips were soft, but there was a dangerous edge to his kiss, as though he was trying to restrain his passion. Skye wasn't about to allow it—not with her. She wanted every part of him, even the ones he kept hidden from the rest of the world.

She ran her hands down his chest, and then slid them up

and under his jacket to touch his heated skin. Nipping at his bottom lip, she said, "Don't hold back, Leo. Not with me."

"You don't know what you're asking," he murmured, unzipping her jacket and pulling it off. "Fuck, Skye, you take me to the edge of all self-control. I want you in every way imaginable."

"Then take me," she demanded, tossing her hair back and looking up at him with a challenge in her eyes. "Or I'll take you."

Her words had their desired effect. Leo spun her around, his hands sliding underneath her shirt. He caressed her stomach, sliding his callused hands over her bare skin. She shivered at his touch, wanting more. He pushed her shirt upward and cupped her breasts. Skye gasped as he ran his thumbs over her sensitive nipples and leaned into his touch.

"Please, Leo," she managed, closing her eyes as his hands explored her body. It had been too long since he'd touched her like this, and she needed him like she needed her next breath. Almost agonizingly slow, he unhooked her UV pants and slid them downward, taking the opportunity to worship every inch of her body with his hands and mouth. Skye trembled at the delicious shivers that went through her as he slowly moved back upward.

"I want to drive you as crazy as you make me," he said, brushing her hair aside and kissing her neck.

"You already do," she whispered, feeling the press of his hardness against her ass. This slow seduction was exquisite torture. Determined to get him to stop teasing her, she started to turn back around, but he grabbed her hands and placed them against the column in front of her.

"Hold on, baby," he said, placing another kiss against her neck. "This is going to be fast and hard. I don't think I can hold back any longer."

She gripped the column, and he fisted her hair, pulling her

tighter against him. With a gasp, she arched her back, feeling him slide inside her welcoming heat. He gripped her hip as he began to move, first slowly and then faster. As the momentum between them built, so did the sensations coursing through her body until she shattered into a thousand pieces. A moment later, Leo withdrew from her body and groaned his own release.

Skye rested her head against the column, trying to catch her breath. Panting softly, she managed, "Wow. You should lose control more often."

Leo chuckled and wrapped his arms around her. She leaned back against him, wishing these moments with him would last forever. He kissed her shoulder and murmured, "I love you, Skye Levanthe."

Her heart soared in response. Every time he said those words, it was a precious gift. Leo had never been one to offer pretty words unless he actually meant them. Skye turned around, searching his expression. The love that shone in his eyes was staggering and overwhelming.

Reaching up to cup his face, she whispered, "I never thought I'd be thankful OmniLab made me leave their trading camp. But having you in my life is better than anything they could have ever offered. I don't want to ever lose you, Leo."

"You won't," he promised and captured her hands in his. "And I don't want to lose you either, which is why we're going to heal your hand *and* help Niko. I'll move heaven and earth to keep you with me, Skye. No matter the cost."

Leo bent down to pick up her jacket. She pulled it on and finished adjusting her clothing. Standing on her toes, she kissed him lightly on his lips.

"I'd do the same for you. Now, come on. Let's go find some shinies for the Omnis."

He chuckled and reached down to grab their bags. She

smiled, wishing they could linger longer. Seeing Leo relaxed and happy didn't happen often enough. Once the storm season passed, they'd have more time alone together. But until then, these moments between them needed to be treasured.

She took her bag from him. "Do you want to try scavenging farther into the building?"

"Yeah. The store next to this one looked promising."

Leo took a handful of steps toward the exit when Skye began to shake. Or rather, something did. She gasped as the ground started trembling beneath her feet. She slipped, falling to the hard floor. Dust and small pieces of debris began falling around them. A scream ripped out of her throat as she struggled to climb to her feet.

Leo grabbed her, tucking her head into the crook of his arm. "Keep your head down!"

She held on to him, unable to see anything, but she heard things falling around them. Deeper within the chasm, she heard the sickly sound of groans and then deafening booms as though buildings were collapsing. It seemed to go on for an eternity, and when the shaking finally stopped, she lifted her head.

Her hands were still trembling as she ran them over Leo's chest, searching for any injuries. His jacket was dusty and torn but that was all she could see. "Are you hurt?"

"No," he said, looking her over too. "Are you okay?"

Skye nodded and glanced toward the exit Leo had mentioned. It looked stable for now, but the thought of heading deeper into the shopping mall made her uneasy. "Maybe that's why people avoid this area. Could the ground be that unstable down here? I don't think the shaking was because of that storm. We haven't seen any flooding."

"I'm not sure," Leo said, standing and helping her to her feet. "I've heard a few stories about people getting turned around or not being able to get through blocked passages. I've never heard any rumors about earthquakes though. I would never have brought you here."

"Find her."

Skye paused, cocking her head. "Did you hear that?"

Leo frowned. "Hear what?"

Skye shook her head and walked toward the exit, trying to listen. "I thought I heard something."

Leo followed her. "It might have been more of the building materials collapsing. If this area is all interconnected like a shopping mall, we run the risk of the whole place coming down. We should get out of here."

"You must find her. Hurry. She needs you."

"There it is again. I don't think—" Her voice cut off as the dim sound of a scream caught her attention. She grabbed Leo's arm. "Someone's out here. They're trapped."

Without waiting for a response, Skye ran out the exit and into a large thoroughfare. Rubble and building debris surrounded her, and she saw what Leo had been talking about. Dozens of store entrances surrounded her, and she listened, trying to determine the direction of the cries. An almost desperate urge to find them filled her, hastening her progress.

"Dammit, Skye," Leo said from behind her. "This is too dangerous. If the ground shakes again, this whole place could come down."

"Hurry, daughter of the sky. She's almost out of time. You cannot let her die."

"We have to help them," she insisted, climbing over a collapsed wall. Urgency flowed through her and some other awareness filled her. She didn't know what she was hearing, but her gut was telling her it was critical to find the people who were trapped. A strange and powerful heat—pure energy

—flowed through her, lending its strength to hers as she raced through the abandoned mall.

"This way," she managed and continued to run, scrambling over fallen debris. The voices and cries grew louder, but they were still too far away. Her blood pounded in her veins, and each pulse was another scream for her to hurry. Leo cursed under his breath, but she knew he was following her. No matter what, Leo always had her back.

"Through there," Leo said, gesturing up a dilapidated staircase. The screams and cries were even closer now.

"It won't open!" a man shouted. "We need to stabilize the ground."

"Everyone with that ability is dead!" a woman yelled. "Try to use your bond to call for help."

Skye skidded into the room, nearly tripping over a fallen structural member. Through a narrow hole, she could see a blond woman bleeding profusely from her head. She couldn't see the man speaking, and there was no way to know who else was alive.

"We can help get you out," Skye called to them, ducking under another beam to try to get closer. It appeared as though most of the room they were in had already collapsed.

"Thank the gods!" The woman moved closer to the hole in the wall. "The whole building is going to collapse."

Leo crouched down, trying to pull the rubble away from the wall. "Start digging it out on your side. Hurry!"

A creak and a groan sounded, and a man screamed somewhere just beyond the wall. The woman's blue eyes were wide with panic. "There's no time. You have to get Kayla to safety."

Before Skye could respond, the woman lifted a dark-haired little girl up into her arms. The child's eyes were wide with fear, and she clung to the woman holding her. Skye stared, shocked at the sight of a child here in the ruins. Their people must have been desperate not only to be scavenging here but to bring a child with them.

Skye reached through the small opening. "She's small enough to fit through. Pass her to me. We'll clear space to get you out too."

Through the hole, Skye saw more dust beginning to fall. The entire floor above them was about to collapse. Once it went, it was only a matter of time before the entire building fell too. She'd seen enough ruins over the years to know that once the structural integrity had been compromised, there was no going back.

The woman whispered something low to the little girl and pushed her toward the hole in the wall. Skye reached through and grabbed the little girl. It was no use; the opening was too small.

"Leo, help me! I can't get her out."

Using his fists and hands, he began breaking apart the wall to widen the hole. The little girl cried out, and Skye yanked her through the opening. Skye stumbled backward, barely managing to catch herself before she fell. Wrapping her arms around the child, she said, "It's okay, sweetheart. I've got you."

The girl's tiny arms clung to her tightly. Skye tried to put her down to help Leo, but the child refused to release her. The woman pressed her hands against the edge of the opening and shouted, "There's no time! Go! Get out of here! Tell Sear—"

The woman's voice turned into a scream as a large beam fell. Skye gasped, turning away to shield the child from the sight.

Leo grabbed her arm. "Go, Skye! We need to get out of here now."

She scrambled back the way they came, hearing more of

the building collapsing from behind them. Leo plucked the child out of her arms. "Run! I'm right behind you!"

Skye nodded and ran, fueled by the knowledge they only had seconds to make it to safety. The pounding of Leo's footsteps behind her urged her onward. Metal screeched, almost sounding like a scream as the building began falling behind them. A cloud of dust exploded around them, obscuring their vision. Skye coughed and choked, the grit in the air burning her eyes and throat. They needed to get out of there.

They ran for their lives, building debris falling around them. When one stumbled, the other helped them up. They abandoned all caution in exchange for speed. They were nearly blind from the dust, the falling building materials creating a maze of debris as they tried to retrace their footsteps while the building fell around them.

Skye skidded back into the first store where she'd found the bracelet and ran to the staircase. Their only hope was that the parking garage was an independent structure. Otherwise, they'd never make it out alive.

CHAPTER SIX

SKYE RAN FARTHER into the garage and dropped to the ground, coughing and choking from the dust burning her lungs. The sound of the buildings collapsing behind them was almost deafening. She blinked furiously, trying to clear the dusty haze from her vision. Leo appeared equally affected, but he'd tried to protect the child by keeping her face buried against his jacket.

The little girl's face was scraped and bleeding, and she wheezed from inhaling the fine dust. Skye fumbled to open the pack at her waist. When she finally got it open, she withdrew a hydrating pack. They needed to get out of there, but it would all be for naught if they couldn't breathe.

"Bring her here," Skye managed, her throat scratchy and sore.

Leo crouched beside her, but the little girl wouldn't release him. Skye scooted closer, pulling out a cloth and pouring some water onto it. Carefully, she began clearing the worst of the dust from around the girl's eyes and nose.

Picking up the hydrating pack, Skye pressed it to the little girl's lips. "You need to drink, sweetheart. It'll help with the dust. Your name's Kayla, right?"

Kayla nodded and wrapped her gloved hands around the hydrating pack, taking a long drink. Relieved, Skye pulled out another one for her and Leo. He shook his head and motioned for her to drink first. She did, the water barely soothing the rawness of her throat. They'd all likely be coughing for a while. Skye splashed some of the water onto the cloth and used it to clear the dust away from her eyes while Leo drank his fill.

Leo coughed. "We need to get out of here. I don't want to take a chance this structure was compromised too. The farther we get from here, the better."

Skye nodded and climbed to her feet. "We don't have a helmet for Kayla. She's small enough that we can hold a bag over her to protect her from the sun, but we'll need to redistribute our supplies or leave them behind."

"We're too low on supplies in camp to risk leaving them here," Leo said, still holding Kayla and glancing around the garage. "If this place goes down, we'll never get them out."

Skye crouched down beside their gear, knowing Leo was right. Yanking open the bag, she quickly pulled out everything and shoved the items into Leo's carrier. When it was empty, she turned toward Kayla. The child was leaning her head against Leo's chest watching her with eyes that were the most striking shade of green Skye had ever seen.

Her heart went out to the little girl. In just a few moments, everything had changed. Skye tilted her head, wondering again about the voice she'd heard. Leo hadn't appeared to hear anything, but it had been so vivid. It was more than a voice, more like a presence that had directed her to Kayla. It couldn't have been her imagination. Something was telling her this child was important somehow.

Skye gave Kayla a small smile. "My name's Skye. The man holding you is Leo. We're going to take care of you until we can find the rest of your camp. Do you know who your camp leader is?"

Kayla's eyes grew wide with panic, and she tightened her arms around Leo. When she buried her head against his chest, Skye frowned and exchanged a worried look with him. For whatever reason, Kayla didn't want to go back to her camp. Unfortunately, they didn't have time to argue the point.

"Hey, kid," Leo started to pull Kayla's arms away from his neck, "you need to tell us where you came from."

"Leo," Skye shook her head, "let's just get to safety. We can figure out the rest later."

"Daryl's going to love that," Leo muttered with a scowl.

Skye frowned, knowing he was right. They didn't have much of a choice though. Daryl would just have to deal with it. She wasn't about to traumatize the little girl even more, given she'd just lost her mother and some of her campmates in a terrible ordeal. If it had been Veridian in Kayla's place, she'd hope the people rescuing him wouldn't abandon him either.

Keeping her tone gentle, Skye said, "Sweetheart, why don't you let me carry you? Leo needs to drive. We'll take you back to our camp and get you cleaned up."

Kayla peeked at her and nodded. She reached out her arms, and Skye lifted her and held her close. She was smaller than Veridian, but not by much. Leo reached down to collect their bags, and Skye ran her hand over the girl's dusty hair.

"See? Everything's going to be fine. You know, I have a little boy about your age. His name is Veridian. I bet he's going to love meeting you."

———

SKYE WAS EXHAUSTED by the time they made it back to camp. Kayla hadn't stopped clinging to her the entire time. She hadn't spoken a word either. Just to make sure she was all right, they'd made several stops so Skye could check on her. The child seemed to be in shock but was otherwise unharmed.

When they pulled up to their camp, Leo reached over to take Kayla from Skye and put her down. Skye rubbed her gloved hand, worried she'd done even more damage in their haste to escape. Little could be done about it now. It wasn't hurting, which was a blessing, but she wouldn't know the extent of the damage until she removed the bandage. They didn't have much to show for their efforts either—only a bracelet, a few coins, and another mouth to feed.

She sighed and climbed off the speeder while Leo started collecting their equipment. The solar cells of the speeder would need to be cleaned, and the rest of their gear would need to be carefully checked before they ventured out again. But all of that needed to wait until they handled the situation with their newest camp addition.

Kayla was busy staring wide-eyed at their camp and vehicles parked out front. Skye cocked her head, wondering how well-off Kayla's camp was if the sight of theirs was so surprising. Even though Kayla's protective gear was ripped and torn, the quality was much better than Skye's. It reminded her of the newer gear she'd received when she worked in Tyler's trading camp.

It was possible Kayla's parents had also worked in a trading camp at one point. Or they could have been making out like bandits scavenging right under the noses of the Omni traders. That might have been why they were in the chasm. Desperation frequently drove people to do daring things— she and Leo were proof of that.

Grabbing one of the bags, Skye threw it over her shoulder

and took Kayla's hand to lead her inside. The girl went willingly enough, seeming content to stay right by her side. Skye placed her helmet on a nearby rack and dropped the bag on the floor. She started pulling off her dusty gear and gestured for Kayla to do the same. More than anything, she wanted a shower and to fall into bed, but all that would have to wait.

Veridian came skidding around the corner, stopping short at the sight of Kayla with them. His eyes widened in confusion, but there was also a trace of excitement. Veridian didn't often get a chance to associate with other children.

Skye managed a smile. "Heya, V. Why don't you come say hi to Kayla? There was an accident in the ruins, and she's going to be here with us until we manage to locate her camp."

"Are you out of your fucking mind?!" Daryl boomed.

Skye frowned as the dark-haired man stormed over to them. Before she could say anything, he said, "I'm not running a damn halfway house. Take her back to wherever you found her or drop her off at a family camp."

Leo's body tensed. Skye reached over, grabbed Kayla, and moved protectively in front of her. Veridian swallowed, and Skye motioned him over too. He ran to her, and she tucked both children behind her.

Leo walked toward Daryl. "A building collapsed. The people she was with were killed, but she's still got people out there. We just have to find them." He gestured to Kayla and added, "Look at her clothing, Daryl. They're good quality. She's well-fed too. She's not some stray from a family camp. Her camp might be willing to barter for her return."

Daryl scowled, glancing toward the children. "And if not? I'm not about to be stuck with another one."

"Give me a few days," Leo said, crossing his arms over his chest. "I'll ask around to see if anyone knows where she belongs. She's even smaller than Veridian. I doubt she'll eat much."

Daryl's jaw clenched. After a long moment, he finally inclined his head. "Fine. You have two days. I want her gone by then." He pointed at Skye. "I'm holding you responsible for her."

Skye nodded, her heart hammering in her chest. Without another word, Daryl turned and headed back down the hall. Two days was better than she'd hoped for. At least they'd have a small reprieve. She sighed in relief and glanced over at Leo's worried expression.

In a quiet voice, Leo said, "He agreed a little too quickly. I don't have a good feeling about this, Skye."

She didn't either, but she couldn't discuss it here and now with him. For Daryl to make the announcement that she was responsible for Kayla didn't bode well. It didn't matter that she would have volunteered. If Daryl was looking for an excuse to throw her out of his camp, he'd just found it. There was no way he'd allow her to keep both children here.

Turning around, she studied both of them. Compared to the children in the family camps, it was obvious Veridian and Kayla were well-cared for. Kayla was dusty and dirty from the ruin collapse, but she didn't have the sunken look to her cheeks that some of the children in the family camps possessed. Her cheeks were tear-streaked, but her eyes were bright. Looking at Veridian and Kayla side by side made it even more apparent they were close to the same age.

Veridian frowned and whispered, "I'm sorry, Mom. I screwed up. The terminal Alanza had me working on broke down. You told me to stay out of trouble, but..." He lowered his head. "I couldn't get it to work again. Daryl got really mad. He's going to make us leave now, isn't he?"

Skye sighed and crouched down to face him. "Look at me, Veridian."

He lifted his head, and her heart clenched at the worry in

his eyes. She reached out to touch his arm. "Equipment is replaceable, yeah?"

"Yeah, but—"

She shook her head. "No. We can fix equipment. We might not know how, but someone does. Or there's some part that needs to be replaced. The trick is finding out the right combination to get it working again."

Veridian frowned. "Alanza said the circuit board was probably fried. She thinks moisture from the storm might have gotten into it."

Skye cocked her head. "Yeah? What do you think?"

He hesitated. "I don't think that's right. None of the other computers had a problem. Wouldn't they have also broken down?"

Kayla stared at Veridian in rapt fascination. It was the first spark of something outside of fear that Skye had seen. She bit back a smile at the girl's interest. "That's very possible. How would you go about troubleshooting it?"

Veridian's expression grew even more serious, and he considered it for a long time. "I'd probably replace each part with pieces from another machine that works. Once I got it working, I'd figure out which part's broken."

"I think that's a good idea," she agreed, squeezing his arm gently. "Let me get cleaned up and help Kayla get situated, and then I'll come help you."

"Are you a fire person?"

Skye paused, surprised by the sound of Kayla's soft voice. It seemed a strange thing to ask, but she gave the young girl a smile. At least she was speaking. That was progress. "What do you mean, sweetheart? Are you cold?"

Kayla's expression became fearful, and she shook her head. Skye glanced up at Leo, but he appeared as perplexed as she felt. Turning back to Kayla, Skye asked, "Would you like to help Veridian and me try to fix the computer?"

Kayla's eyes widened. "Me? You'll let me help?"

"Sure. Between the three of us, I bet we can figure out the problem. Besides, your small hands will be much better than mine at taking apart the system. Have you ever taken apart a computer system?"

Kayla shook her head.

Skye smiled. As far as distractions went, it would be sufficient for now. "Well, I'm sure you'll be an expert soon enough. Let's get cleaned up first. You can wear some of Veridian's spare clothes, then we can tackle the computer problem."

Veridian grinned at Kayla. "Chance lets me use his special tools, but I'll bet he'll let you try them out too. Chance is really cool. You'll like him."

When Skye stood, Leo leaned in close and whispered, "Be careful, baby. I'll go talk to Chance and see what happened while we were gone. Keep the kids away from Daryl as much as possible."

Skye nodded. She'd do her best, but Daryl had a way of turning up at the worst possible moments. Taking Kayla and Veridian's hands in hers, she led her young wards down the corridor, hoping she could protect all of them from whatever Fate had in store.

———

A SOFT WHIMPER WOKE SKYE. Reaching over, she put her hand on Kayla's back and the child stilled. She waited until Kayla's breathing was once again deep and regular before removing her hand. This was at least the fourth time that night she'd awakened, but it was impossible to begrudge Kayla for her nightmares. The trauma of the building collapse earlier would probably continue to plague the child for a long time. It would have been hard enough for an adult to handle, but to a child, such scars might never heal.

She listened, but it didn't sound like Kayla had disturbed anyone else. Light snores and other nighttime noises filled the room as the majority of their camp slept. Niko and a few others who had been injured had been moved to another part of the building. A few people were awake in other parts of the camp to monitor them and also to watch for emergencies or possible thieves. Everyone else tended to congregate in one main room while they slept. It helped conserve energy and resources, especially since part of the building had been damaged during the storm. She and Leo had pulled their sleeping mats to the far corner of the room, and both children were sleeping beside them.

Leo wrapped his arms around her and murmured, "You need to get some sleep too, baby."

"So do you," she whispered, burrowing against his chest. In the relative darkness, she could enjoy such small intimacies with him. He stroked her back, seemingly content to hold her. He often did this when something was troubling him, and she didn't have to be a mind reader to know what it was.

While they were gone trying to scavenge for artifacts, the rest of their people had returned from being stranded during the storm. There were a few more injuries, but thankfully, no one had died. Skye's risky attempt at getting a message to their people had worked, but now they were facing more challenges. The few tradeable items their campmates had brought back weren't nearly enough to cover the camp's supply deficit. Daryl had been on the warpath ever since. She'd barely had a few moments to catch her breath before tumbling into bed.

After several minutes, Leo sighed and kissed her hair. In a quiet voice, he said, "I should get up and head out. Do you mind getting up with me? I want to check your hand before I leave. We didn't have a chance earlier."

She made a noise of agreement and got up, leaving the children sleeping on the floor in their makeshift beds. Keeping her footsteps quiet, she followed Leo down the hall and into a room where some of their storage was being kept. Most of the crates were empty, another reminder of their dwindling supplies and the pressing need to acquire more resources soon.

Leo turned around. "I won't be gone longer than the two days Daryl gave us. I'll try to hit as many camps as possible to see if anyone knows anything about Kayla's camp. While I'm gone, try to keep the kids away from Daryl. If he doesn't see them, he won't think about them quite so much."

Skye arched a brow. "You think it's possible to hide a couple of kids that age in a camp this size?"

Leo grinned. "If anyone's creative enough to do it, you are."

Skye smiled and moved closer. "I'll see what I can do. But I won't abandon her to a family camp, Leo. She's an innocent child. You know what could happen to her there."

Leo's expression turned grim, and he ran a hand over his short hair. "I know. We'll figure it out. Hopefully, she has someone who will take her in."

Skye frowned and didn't say anything right away.

Leo lifted her chin to look into her eyes. "What is it?"

"There's something about her," Skye admitted, biting her lip. "When we were down in those ruins, I thought I heard a voice telling me she needed me."

Leo's brow furrowed. "Her mother? She asked you to take her to safety."

Skye shook her head. "No. It was before we even discovered them. It felt like something was leading us to them. And when I look at Kayla, I get the feeling I need to protect her.

She was frightened at the thought of being returned to her camp. I can't help but believe she's supposed to be here... with us."

Leo was quiet for a long time. "I've never discounted your hunches, baby. I'd be a fool to start now. If I find her camp, I'll see what the situation is before we agree to anything."

Her shoulders relaxed, and Skye nodded. She trusted Leo's judgment implicitly. Placing her hands against Leo's bare chest, she felt the reassuring rhythm of his heartbeat under her fingertips. "Be safe when you're out there. I don't want anything to happen to you either."

Leo cupped her face and murmured, "I hate leaving you here alone, especially knowing our supplies are so limited. Daryl's getting desperate, and I'm worried about what he might do. If we can get some of our people out scavenging soon, maybe we can turn things around."

"We'll be fine here," she said gently, giving him a small smile. "You just focus on finding Kayla's camp. The supplies will get sorted. We always bounce back from this stuff."

Leo nodded. "I talked to Chance earlier. He'll try to run interference if things get bad, but Daryl doesn't usually listen to him. He won't be able to do much without risking his place here."

"I'll be fine," she promised, standing on her toes and pressing a light kiss against his lips. "Just come back to me soon. I always miss you when you're gone."

Leo wrapped his arms around her, drawing her close. He leaned down to nuzzle her neck and murmured, "Fuck, Skye. I have a bad feeling about leaving you here."

She traced a pattern against his chest, comforted by his surrounding warmth. "I tried asking Kayla about her camp a little bit. She won't talk about them and shuts down any time I bring it up. But the woman in the ruins was probably her mother. When we were down there, the woman said a partial name: 'See-air'. Maybe someone will know who she was talking about. It might be their camp leader."

"I'll see what I can find out. I have a few contacts in other camps who might have heard something. Maybe they'll also have some medical supplies for your hand. We should have cleaned it as soon as we got back."

Leo reached down and captured her bandaged hand. Skye frowned, watching as he carefully unwound the wrapping.

"I don't understand," she whispered, staring at her unblemished palm in shock. "How is this possible?"

Leo frowned, his gaze darting up to meet hers before lowering to her hand again. "This couldn't be from the metabolic booster. We would have seen effects before now, and nothing this dramatic. Has it been bothering you at all?"

She shook her head. "Not since we were in the ruins."

His frown deepened. "Did you touch anything down there?"

"No. I was wearing my gloves the entire time, but..." Her voice trailed off as she remembered running in the ruins and the strange sensation that had flowed through her. "Do you think it's possible that whatever directed us to Kayla was also responsible for healing my hand? I felt a warmth when we were running toward them."

Leo ran his fingertips over her palm. "I don't know. I've heard about weird things happening there, but nothing like this. Maybe I should go back with Chance when things settle down and check it out. If there's something down there that can heal an injury that severe—"

A strange chill settled over her, and goose bumps broke out along her skin. Skye shook her head at the sense of wrongness pounding inside her chest. The thought of Leo going back there terrified her. She'd never have survived this long if she hadn't learned to trust her instincts. "No. We need to stay away from that chasm."

When he hesitated, Skye gripped his arms. It was more than just her worry about the earth shaking, but she wasn't sure she could describe everything she'd experienced down there. "Please, Leo. I can't explain it, but I need you to promise me you'll stay away. You can't go back there. Not now."

"Hey," Leo took her hands in his again, "I won't go. If it worries you that much, I'll stay away."

She bit her lip and nodded. "I don't think we should tell anyone either. They might want to go down there themselves, and I think that would be dangerous."

"You're probably right," he mused, turning her palm upward again and running his thumb across it. "If anyone asks, we'll say the metabolic booster worked better than we expected."

She blew out a relieved breath and nodded. "I think that would be best."

"Whatever the reason for this, I'm just hoping it healed clean." Leo lifted her hand and placed a kiss against it. "Try resting your hand as much as possible over the next couple of days, just in case."

Touched by the sweet gesture, Skye smiled up at him. "You can't help but worry, can you?" Before he could respond, she kissed him lightly. "I'll be fine. Just concentrate on finding Kayla's camp. I'll take care of everything here."

A sound from somewhere within the camp made her turn. It didn't sound like Kayla, but she could wake up at any moment. Skye frowned. "I should get back to the kids before Kayla wakes anyone."

"Skye, wait," Leo said, pulling her tightly against him.

He fisted his hand in her hair as he claimed her mouth. She let out a moan, meeting his need with hers, and poured every ounce of her worry and fear into that kiss. It was impossible to know what tomorrow might bring, so they needed to treat each moment together like their last. She'd learned at an early age never to let the people she loved walk away without letting them know how she felt.

"I'll be back as quick as I can, baby," Leo promised. "Now that your hand's healed, I want both of them on me again—and soon."

She smiled up at him. "Then hurry. I want that too."

CHAPTER SEVEN

SKYE WRUNG out the cooling cloth and leaned forward, pressing it gently against Niko's face. He mumbled something incoherent and tossed his head as though trying to escape. Skye frowned. Not even sleep was a deterrent from the pain chasing him.

She dipped the cooling cloth back into the water and wrung out the excess moisture again. Niko had been steadily getting worse. Despite their best efforts, it was unlikely he'd recover. The only thing they could do was to try to make him as comfortable as possible.

Alanza was sitting across from her, and the young woman's eyes were red and weary. She'd barely left Niko's side since he'd been injured. Skye could relate; if it had been Leo in Niko's position, nothing would have prevented her from being there for him.

"Daryl offered Niko something to stop his heart," Alanza whispered, taking Niko's hand in hers again. "I'm not ready to say goodbye to him yet, Skye. I don't want to lose him."

Skye sighed and ran the cloth over Niko's arms. "I know,

but this decision belongs to Niko. He's in a lot of pain, and the tonic is barely touching the worst of it."

"That's just it. Daryl hasn't really tried to help him," Alanza retorted, her eyes welling with angry tears. "He's just anxious for me to get back to work. He told me Niko's taking up a lot of time and valuable resources. You, Leo, and Chance are the only ones who truly care."

Skye winced and dipped the cloth again. Daryl had never been the most tactful person, but he wasn't evil. They simply didn't have the resources available to help Niko. Unfortunately, there wasn't anything she could say to Alanza that would make this situation better. With a sigh, Skye ran the cloth over Niko's other arm. At least he'd stopped thrashing in his sleep and appeared to be resting a little easier now.

Alanza sniffled. "That seems to have helped. How long will he sleep?"

"Not long," Skye admitted, folding the cloth and placing it beside Niko. "We might have an hour or two before the tonic wears off and he wakes again. If you want to get some rest, I can stay with him for a while."

Alanza shook her head. "I appreciate it, but I can't leave him. I need to be here in case he wakes up. I don't want Daryl to push him into anything. Maybe Leo's been delayed because he found a lead on a bone mold and medicine."

A lump formed in Skye's throat, and she didn't respond. They both knew it was a false hope, but Alanza desperately wanted to believe it. Skye wouldn't take that away from her. The time for hard truths was rapidly approaching, and no one could cheat Fate.

"Try giving Niko more of the tonic when he wakes up," Skye said, picking up the bottle to gauge the amount that was left. Unfortunately, they were nearly out. She'd have to make another batch soon, but that would require a trip outside OmniLab territory to gather the ingredients.

When she was growing up in one of the family camps, her mother had taught her to make the tonic with some of the plants that grew nearby. It wasn't as effective as OmniLab's medicine, but it was helpful for minor ailments. They'd been giving larger doses of it to Niko to allow him a bit of rest, but the effects were minimal. It had never been intended for such serious injuries.

Alanza nodded but didn't look away from Niko. Skye stood and quietly left the room, her heart breaking at the pain in Alanza's eyes. The minute Skye was outside, she leaned against the wall. Tears filled her eyes, and she hastily wiped them away. No matter how many times people she cared about were hurt, it never got any easier.

Taking a steadying breath, Skye headed down the hallway in search of the children. After sitting in the room with Niko and witnessing his suffering, she desperately wanted to hold her son and reassure herself he was safe. The sound of Veridian and Kayla's voices caught her attention, and she headed toward the room where they'd moved some of their computer equipment.

They were sitting on the floor together, and Veridian was showing Kayla some of the tools spread out on the floor near them. Skye paused for a moment, watching as the next generation of ruin rats worked side by side. With a pang, Skye realized one day something might happen to her too, just like it had with Niko. Veridian would be left alone, without anyone to guide him—just like Kayla had been abandoned.

Pushing aside her dark thoughts, Skye walked over to them. "It sounds like you two have been busy in here. What's going on?"

Veridian beamed a smile at her, making her heart hurt a little at the innocence in his eyes. "Kayla wants to learn how to fix the computer. I'm going to teach her. Chance said we could work on this one."

Skye arched her brow and sat on the ground. "Not a bad idea. Walk me through it. What's the first step?"

Veridian frowned, his expression turning serious as he studied the computer in front of him. "We have to make sure there's no power going to the unit before we take off the cover."

Skye made a small noise of approval, watching while Veridian checked the connections. He showed Kayla how to adjust it, and Skye only needed to make a few minor corrections to his explanation.

Once he'd finished, Veridian turned to Kayla. "Ready for the next part? We're going to take it apart."

Kayla's eyes lit up, and she nodded. Skye leaned back and watched them. Kayla still wasn't talking much. She seemed to have an almost insatiable desire to learn, absorbing every detail around her. The only one Kayla seemed to open up with was Veridian, and he'd taken her under his wing to tell her everything he could about their camp.

As the only child within the camp, Veridian was only used to interacting with other adults. This experience was good for him, and Skye suspected it was helping Kayla with some of her grief. At least, she hoped. It would be better once Kayla was reunited with her former camp, assuming everything checked out okay with them. But if Skye was honest, she'd miss Kayla. She'd already begun to develop a strong affection for her foster daughter. Her intuition was telling her Kayla was supposed to be here with them—at least for now.

It had been three days since Leo had left, and no one had heard anything from him. Worry was beginning to set in. He should have been back by now. A hundred things could have happened to him. If his speeder broke down or he got caught in a storm, there was no way to track him. That was one of the reasons they usually traveled in pairs. But Skye couldn't risk leaving the children alone with Daryl, especially since he was eager to get rid of them. She wasn't even sure where to start looking for Leo.

"Yeah, now we just slide off the cover," Veridian said to Kayla, showing her how to remove it.

"That's it?"

Veridian nodded. He reached into Chance's toolkit and frowned. "I don't know where the testing meter went. Did you see it?"

Skye glanced around the floor but didn't see any sign of it. "Chance may have taken it with him to work on some of the outside equipment. He was going to find an alternate site to mount the new antenna."

Veridian shook his head. "No. He was helping Daryl move some crates. He said he wouldn't need any of his tools this afternoon." Veridian's frown deepened. "I can't lose it, Mom. Chance trusted me with all his tools. I don't want to let him down."

Skye put her hand over Veridian's and squeezed it gently. "We'll find it, V. It's got to be around here somewhere. Maybe it just didn't make it back into his kit."

She stood and started checking around the communication equipment. Chance was usually pretty organized, but it could have been accidentally misplaced. With everything being moved around after the storm, nothing was where it should be.

Kayla bit her lip. "What does the testing meter look like?"

"It's about this big." Veridian held out his hands to indicate the size. "It has dials on it and a solar cell on the top for power. There's a big scratch on the side from when Chance dropped it. He says it's his lucky testing meter because it didn't break."

Kayla's brow furrowed in concentration. A cool chill swept over Skye, and she idly rubbed the goose bumps prickling her arms.

Kayla pointed to the other side of the room. "I think it's on the floor behind that crate."

Skye paused, glancing in the direction Kayla indicated. There was no sign of the testing meter from where she was standing, but her instincts warned her it was there. Skye walked over to the crate and leaned over to peer behind it. There, wedged between the wall and the floor, was the testing meter.

Reaching into the narrow crevice, she pulled out the device. It should have been impossible. If Kayla hadn't told them where it was, they likely wouldn't have found it for days or even weeks. Skye turned around to find Kayla watching her with a worried expression.

"You found it!" Veridian rushed over to Skye to retrieve the piece of equipment.

Careful to keep her voice quiet so no one outside the room could overhear, Skye asked, "How did you know it was there, Kayla?"

Kayla's eyes widened, a look of guilt on her face, but she didn't answer. Veridian frowned and held the testing meter against his chest.

Skye walked over to Kayla and crouched down in front of her. "You're not in any trouble, sweetheart. Can you tell me how you knew it was there?"

Kayla shook her head, her expression growing panicked. Skye frowned. The last thing Skye wanted to do was frighten Kayla. In an effort to reassure her, Skye reached over to take Kayla's small hand. The little girl was trembling.

Skye hesitated, not wanting to upset Kayla any further—she'd been through so much. Maybe sharing something about herself might help. "Can I tell you a secret, Kayla? It's something only Veridian and one other person knows."

In a shaky voice, Kayla asked, "What secret?"

Skye smiled and ran her thumb over Kayla's hand. "Sometimes, I get feelings about people or things. I don't like to tell anyone because a lot of them don't understand."

Kayla's eyes widened. "You do?"

Skye nodded. "That's how I found you that day in the ruins. Something led me to you. I knew I had to find you and protect you. I've always told Veridian it's important to trust your instincts. Sometimes, it doesn't make sense, but it usually works out in the end."

"You heard it too," Kayla whispered. "The voice said you'd protect me."

Skye froze. It wasn't possible. She swallowed. "You heard a voice in the ruins?"

"I wanted to find it for Daddy," Kayla whispered, her eyes shimmering with tears. "But now he's gone too. They're all gone. It's all my fault. I miss my mommy and daddy."

Skye's heart clenched at the pain in Kayla's eyes. "Oh, sweetheart," she murmured, reaching out to hug Kayla. The little girl threw her arms around her neck, and Skye's heart broke just a little more. She ran her hand over Kayla's hair and held her as she cried. "It's not your fault, Kayla. What happened could never be your fault."

"Mom?" Veridian took a step toward them.

Skye reached out her other arm and wrapped it around Veridian. He leaned against her and patted Kayla's back in a reassuring gesture.

"Don't cry, Kayla. Look..." Veridian held up the testing meter in his hand. "Wanna learn how to use it?"

Kayla sniffed and turned her head to blink up at Veridian. She rubbed her eyes. "You'll show me? Chance won't get mad?"

Veridian shook his head. He handed Kayla the testing meter. "Chance is my friend. I bet he'll be your friend too."

Skye blinked back her tears and gently tousled Veridian's hair. It was just like her son to try to fix things, including hurt feelings. He had such a good heart. She hoped he'd never have cause to harden it.

Kayla sniffled again and took the testing meter. "Okay. What do I do?"

Veridian turned the dials on the face of the testing meter. "It's not hard. The machine does most of the work. We just have to test all the different pieces in the computer to find the bad one. Rebuilding it is the best part. Chance usually lets me use his tools. One day, I'll get my own."

Kayla studied the testing meter in her hand. "Will I get my own tools too one day?"

Skye smiled and tucked Kayla's loose hair behind her ear. "If that's what you want, I'm sure we can figure something out. You'll need to become really good at using them first."

Kayla nodded, a look of determination in her eyes. "I will."

"Then we'll make it happen," Skye promised.

Kayla stared down at the testing meter. "How do you know it's telling the truth?"

Skye arched a brow. "What do you mean?"

Kayla looked up at her, her eyes still shining with her recently shed tears. "How do you know the meter is working right? If it says a part is bad, how do you know it's telling the truth? Does... does it ever lie?"

Skye paused, wondering if Kayla was asking about something more than just the testing meter. "That's a really good question," Skye admitted with a small smile. She had the impression Kayla could use a distraction right about now, and she had a perfect one. "Equipment doesn't lie, but it can stop working properly. We run calibration tests to make sure it's telling us the truth. But you brought up a good point. That testing meter you're holding is probably due for another check. Veridian, why don't you show Kayla how to make sure it's working properly before you start troubleshooting the components?"

"Aw, Mom," Veridian grumbled.

Skye's smile deepened. "Kayla should know how to do this if she's going to be an expert one day. Besides, if she learns how to do it, that will be one less responsibility for you."

Veridian's eyes lit up, and he motioned for Kayla to follow him. "Come on, Kayla. I'll show you. The calibration equipment is in the other room."

Skye stood just as footsteps sounded behind her.

"Skye, I need a word with you."

She tensed at the sound of Daryl's voice. Turning around, she saw Daryl and Alanza had entered the room. Skye glanced over at the children, but Alanza shook her head in warning. Daryl must have specifically asked her to leave Niko's side to watch the children. An unmistakable trace of pity was in Alanza's eyes as she offered, "I'll keep an eye on them while you're talking to Daryl."

Skye frowned and nodded, turning to follow Daryl into the other room. He led her into the small room he'd been using as his private area. Chance was already inside, which only reaffirmed her suspicions. He leaned against the wall, an apology in his eyes as he regarded her. Well, that cleared things up. At least now she knew why Daryl wanted to speak with her.

She ignored Chance and turned back to Daryl, waiting for him to begin this conversation. They both knew why he'd brought her in here, but she didn't intend to make this easy on him.

Daryl sighed. "It's been three days, Skye. Leo's not back yet. We don't know if something happened to him, but we need to assume the worst."

"Don't," she said, a lump forming in her throat. She couldn't think such a thing. The thought of a life without Leo was unfathomable. If Leo was still alive, he'd return to her. Until she had confirmation otherwise, she had to believe he was okay. "Leo *will* be back."

Daryl fell silent for a long time. "I hope you're right, but I can't delay this any longer." He gestured to Chance and added, "Chance is going to take Kayla to one of the family camps. If Leo comes back, we can let her camp know where we've taken her."

"Fuck that," Skye said, straightening and darting her gaze back and forth between the men. "You think I'm going to make this easy on you? You can't send her there. She'll never survive without someone to look after her. She's just a child."

Daryl's eyes narrowed. "I can't keep her here. I know you care about her, but she's not your responsibility. As it is, we've already taken on the burden of helping you with Veridian. With both of those kids here, you haven't been out to scavenge anything for days."

"I *paid* you to allow me to keep Veridian here," she reminded him, her tone sharper than it should have been, but how dare he insinuate her son was a burden. Veridian helped out in the camp as much as possible. The older he got, the more he'd continue to contribute. "And I've been working nonstop over the past several days taking care of our injured and repairing equipment, including that old cooling unit we thought was defunct."

"I don't need more techs," Daryl snapped. "I need scavengers who aren't busy babysitting some snot-nosed brats. If you can't help us find items to trade, I can't keep this camp running. Those artifacts keep us fed. That's what you promised me when I took you on, Skye."

"Then I'll go back into the ruins. Put me on the roster tomorrow with Chance. Alanza will watch the kids for me."

Daryl crossed his arms over his chest. "Alanza's taking care of Niko, and she's got her own problems with me. Face it, Skye, the girl's got to go. I can't have two children running around my scavenging camp. If they were older, I could put them to work, but they're just a drain on our supplies."

"It's for the best, Skye," Chance added. "She's not your kid. Don't take on the responsibility for her."

Skye took a steadying breath, a cold chill flooding through her at the thought of sending Kayla away. She wouldn't be able to live with herself if she abandoned Kayla to one of those camps. "If you're that determined to get rid of her, I'll take her to the family camp."

"Good." Daryl walked over to a crate he'd been using as a table. "Chance can drop her off. I'll put you on the schedule with him tomorrow to go back into the ruins, but I want results from both of you. We're too far behind, especially now with Leo missing."

"No."

Daryl lifted his head and narrowed his eyes on her. "This isn't a negotiation."

"I'm not negotiating. You're misunderstanding," she said, putting her hands on her hips. "I'll take Veridian *and* Kayla to the family camp, but I'm staying with them until Leo gets back. She's already lost her family. I will *not* abandon an innocent little girl."

"Out of the question. If you walk out that door, you're gone for good," Daryl warned in a low voice. "I won't take you back."

Chance pushed away from the wall, his eyes wide. "You can't want this, Skye. Leo would go out of his mind if he knew you were thinking about walking away. Don't give up your life and Veridian's life here over this."

Ignoring Chance, Skye lifted her chin and took a step toward Daryl. "If we're the type of people who would be willing to do this to a defenseless child, then it just shows how far we've fallen. Survival is about more than putting food in our bellies. The soul can wither and die too." She gestured toward the door. "That child out there—both of those children—they're our future. We're setting the example they're going to spend their lives following. If we don't show them compassion and teach them to be better than this, we're dooming all of us. I will *not* be a part of this."

Daryl's jaw clenched. "So be it. Chance can drop all three of you off."

Chance frowned, his gaze darting back and forth between them. "Daryl, maybe we can give Leo a few more days. We need Skye here, especially with so many of our people hurt. She's a damned good scavenger and you know it."

Daryl scowled. "If you want to join them at the family camp, go ahead. I need people in this camp who will follow orders. If you want to hold on to your pathetic ideals, leave. I have dozens of people who would give up anything to be a part of this camp. You're all replaceable."

"Chance, let it go," Skye said, unwilling to let him get thrown out too. Other than Leo, Chance was the best scavenger they had. She wouldn't let him sacrifice himself because of a promise he'd made to Leo on her behalf. "I'll get my things and be gone within the hour."

"Chance will drop the three of you off with the cargo vehicle," Daryl said, turning back to his tablet.

Skye paused, her eyes narrowing. "I'm taking a speeder."

Daryl lifted his head again. "You don't have a speeder to take, Skye."

She glared at him and took a step toward him. "I came here with a speeder. I intend to take one with me when I leave."

"You signed over everything to me when you came here," Daryl reminded her. "That speeder belongs to me. You can take your personal possessions, but that's it."

Skye clenched her fists. Without a vehicle, she couldn't

even escape from the family camp without depending on someone else or stealing from someone less fortunate. She'd hoped to at least have the ability to scavenge and buy additional supplies from a trading camp. "You have no right, Daryl."

Daryl's gaze hardened. "I have every right. You made the offer eight years ago. I simply accepted it. You can't change the terms of that agreement now. If you don't like it, that's too damn bad. Leaving with those kids is your choice. Stay or not, but the girl goes and the speeder stays."

Skye held his gaze for a long moment, understanding immediately why he was doing this. By refusing to allow her a speeder, he was trying to force her into accepting his terms. He'd sorely miscalculated her determination and the consequences of his decision though.

When Leo returned, he'd be furious when he found out Daryl had forced this issue. Over the past few years, many of the people in the camp had begun following Leo. The leadership in the camp was already beginning to shift. Many of them now came to Leo for direction before turning to Daryl. Leo may not be pushing for it yet, but Daryl had to know his days were numbered. If he risked alienating Leo, those days might be even fewer.

Daryl wasn't a fool. He knew how Leo felt about her. Even though she and Leo had tried to be discreet, the camp was too small for people not to pick up on certain intimacies. Daryl most likely didn't care if Skye stayed or went, except to keep his position secure. In fact, he'd probably prefer she was gone. With Leo's absence, many people in the camp were turning to her instead. And she didn't have the same respect or loyalty toward Daryl that Leo possessed.

Her mouth curved in a small smile, just enough to let Daryl know they understood one another. "Enjoy the speeder,

Daryl. I suspect you may be the one needing it more once Leo gets back."

Without saying another word, she turned and headed out of the room to collect her belongings.

Chance jogged after her. "Skye, I'm sorry. I asked him to wait, but—"

She held up her hand to stop him. "Don't. I appreciate what you tried to do in there, but it's not up to any of us. It was just a matter of time before Daryl kicked me out anyway. We all knew this was coming. At least I go on my terms this way."

"It's not right," he said quietly.

"No, it's not," she agreed, walking into the crew's quarters. They didn't have much as far as possessions went, but she'd take what she could. Heading over to her bed, she pulled out her scavenging bag.

Chance crouched down beside her. "You don't have to do this. We can figure out something else. Maybe if I talk to some of the others—"

"The decision's been made. This isn't your fight."

Chance frowned. "I can't stop you, can I?"

She paused, tilting her head to regard him. "No, but I appreciate the thought. I meant what I said. I won't abandon Kayla."

His shoulders slumped, and he nodded. "I know it's not much, but I'll bring you supplies whenever I can. And as soon as Leo gets back, I'll tell him where you went. He won't let you stay there."

Skye gave him a small smile and started rolling up her sleeping mat. "If Leo were able to come back, he would have already been here by now. You know that." She paused, lowering her head, and tried to ignore her breaking heart. She didn't want to stay here if Leo was truly gone. She would have left Daryl's camp a long time ago if it weren't for Leo.

Blinking back the tears that threatened to fall, she focused on collecting her belongings.

Chance sighed and pulled out his knife. He held it out to her hilt first and said, "Take it. Do what you need to do to survive."

She nodded and accepted the blade, touched he'd given her such a valuable gift. Leaning over, she kissed his cheek. "I always have, Chance."

CHAPTER EIGHT

DESPAIR AND SICKNESS had a distinctive smell, and it permeated the air of the family camp. The pungent stench wafted out from some of the buildings in the old converted town. Buildings had been retrofitted to provide some measure of temporary shelter, but it was clear this was a place that afforded little.

Chance frowned at her. "Skye, maybe we can—"

She gave him a curt shake of her head. "It's fine. Get gone, Chance. I can't have you here."

He hesitated, and she shot him a warning look. It was going to be difficult enough to find a place here, but if they thought she had friends in the scavenging camps, people would be drawn to her for all the wrong reasons. Although, there weren't many right ones.

Chance gave her a nod and walked toward the cargo vehicle. She ignored him and motioned for Veridian and Kayla to keep close. On the way to the family camp, she'd given them warnings to make themselves as unobtrusive as possible. Skye hefted the heavy bag over her shoulder and headed deeper into the family camp. Her other hand rested on the knife at her side as her gaze swept over the people they passed.

She'd learned in her early years to pay close attention to the surroundings but try to remain part of the background. Unfortunately, any time there were new arrivals in a camp, all attention shifted to them. They were already being sized up, and Skye knew they were noting their better-quality clothing and healthier pallor. It was a clear sign they weren't simply transplants from another family camp.

A woman with a hardened expression leaned against one of the buildings and crossed her arms as they approached. She was most likely a handful of years older than Skye, but her cheeks were sunken and her eyes tired, giving her the appearance of being much older.

Skye paused and arched her brow. "You have room?"

The woman spat into the dirt. "Just the three of you, or is your man coming back?"

"Drop off only." Skye tightened her hand around the hilt of the knife. "He's not my man."

"Ain't that the way of it," the woman muttered, glancing down at Veridian and Kayla. "Your kids appear pretty healthy. We don't have much, but you're welcome to a place."

Skye glanced around and noted several others were paying close attention to the conversation. A few had moved closer, most likely also sizing her up or listening in. She didn't know this woman's position here, but the fact they were close to the entrance indicated hers was more advantageous than others. "We don't have much either, but we can share what we've got. How many are here?"

The woman assessed her shrewdly. "Best you come inside. You keep walking farther into camp and you're gonna attract more attention than you want. Unless you have kin here, no one will lift a hand when some of our boys try to steal you blind."

Without saying a word, the woman turned and ducked inside. Skye pursed her lips and led Veridian and Kayla into the structure. It was darker within the small building, but the stifling heat made it apparent why the woman had been outside. At first glance, Skye spotted two other adults and three children. One of the women had a baby pressed against her breast while the two other children played some sort of game in the corner. An older man slept on a nearby pallet.

The woman gestured to an area of the room where some debris had been pushed aside. "You can set up over in that corner."

Skye nodded and walked over to where she indicated, putting the heavy bag on the ground. "I appreciate it. I'm Skye, and this is Veridian and Kayla."

The woman nodded. "The name's Tali." She motioned to the woman with the infant. "That's Bridge taking care of old Pete. And over there," she indicated the two children who were now staring at Kayla and Veridian, "that's Gryph and Cayenne."

Skye gave them all a nod. It took only a few seconds to take the pulse of the room. Tali was more or less in charge for the time being, but based on the number of pallets, a handful more were wandering the camp. She'd wait to see who else would reappear later to determine whether or not they stuck around.

A weak cough caught her attention, and she glanced over at the older man. From the raspy breathing and rattle in his chest, it didn't sound good.

Tali noticed and said, "We don't think it's catching."

Skye didn't respond. All things considered, they were fortunate more of the people here weren't sick. She crouched down to open the bag and withdrew one of the sleeping mats. Rolling it out, she motioned for Veridian and Kayla to help her with it. Judging by Kayla's pale face and wide eyes, the little girl needed a job to distract her from the surroundings. Veridian was equally wary, but he'd traveled with her before to the family camp. Skye wasn't sure if Kayla had ever spent time in one.

Skye turned toward Tali. "Is there a water collection place nearby?"

"You armed?"

When Skye nodded, Tali gestured to the older boy. "Gryph, go show them to the well."

Skye hesitated. If she took Veridian and Kayla with her, their belongings would remain unprotected. Until she knew these people better, she couldn't risk it.

Kayla still appeared a little shell-shocked, and Skye didn't know how well she'd handle herself in a difficult situation. At least Leo had been working with Veridian a bit on self-defense. She'd never been more thankful for the lessens than now.

Crouching down, she withdrew her other knife from her boot and handed it hilt first to Veridian. "I need you to stay here. I'll be back in ten minutes. Can you do that for me?"

Veridian swallowed but accepted the knife. He sat on the mat, leaning against the wall so he could watch the entire room. "I'm fine, Mom. You can trust me."

Tali's eyes lit up in approval. "You've got yourself a good little man there."

Skye glanced over at Gryph, who was waiting to take them to the well. He appeared to be a few years older than Veridian, probably closer to eleven or twelve. Skye guessed he'd probably be out trying to make a living for himself scavenging in another year or two. They always started young, but skill and luck depended on how long they'd survive. Turning back to Tali, she asked, "Is Gryph your boy?"

Tali paused, her eyes narrowing slightly. "Yes."

"He just as good?"

Tali's mouth curved upward. "You've got spunk, I'll give you that much. With those fancy-ass clothes, I was wondering if you'd gone soft in one of those scavenging camps."

Skye inclined her head. "We all come from the same roots, and we all end up in the same place. You take care of me and mine, Tali, and I'll do the same for you."

Tali held her gaze for a long moment, her brown eyes sharp. They weren't so far off in age, and except for a twist in Fate, Skye could have been the one standing in Tali's shoes.

Finally, Tali nodded. "Done. If you run into Hobb and his crew, keep your weapon handy."

Skye didn't know who this Hobb was, but there were always a few troublemakers in every camp. Crouching down beside Kayla, she said, "You need to stay right with me, yeah?"

Kayla nodded, darting a quick glance at Veridian as though worried about leaving him. Skye reached into the bag to pull out the large canteen they'd brought with them. In the scavenging camp, they typically reused hydrating packs they purchased from OmniLab, but she couldn't keep running back and forth to the well to refill the few she had.

Skye handed Kayla the canteen. "You're gonna need to carry that for me. Veridian will be fine. Just stay close to me. We'll be back soon." She leaned close to Kayla and whispered, "He knows how to use that weapon. I'll teach you too."

Kayla's eyes widened. "Promise?"

Skye smiled. "Promise. Now come on."

She stood and followed Gryph outside with Kayla sticking right by her side. At least Kayla followed instructions well, and it allowed Skye to keep her hand on her weapon. The gravel crunched underneath her feet from asphalt that had worn away years ago. When she'd lived in the trader camp, she'd watched some videos showing what the world had been like before the war. Part of her wondered if the people back then would have chosen their same path if they had any idea how much they'd destroy. Maybe that had been their intention. She'd probably never know, not that it mattered much now.

A loud buzzing indicated the UV guard over the area was still working, which was promising considering there were some family camps that didn't have even that much. Barriers were marked off with warning signs indicating the areas where it was safe to walk. Daytime was usually a time for sleep, while darkness tended to afford more protection from the elements. It was the opposite in the trading and scavenging camps, where expensive technology had created more flexible schedules. It would probably take a while to adjust to being nocturnal.

Night was starting to fall, and people were beginning to emerge from their homes. She continued walking quickly, intent to get back before any unwelcome visitors stopped by Tali's place. The area between her shoulder blades started to itch from the number of people watching them. She placed her hand on Kayla's shoulder, hugging the girl toward her while her other hand gripped the knife tightly.

Kayla was a pretty child, which wasn't exactly conducive to keeping a low profile. But Skye was determined to protect her with her last breath, just as she would with Veridian. She believed what she'd told Daryl back at the scavenging camp. These children were their future, and she was determined to make sure they survived to see it.

————

LEO WALKED into the camp and dropped his bag on the floor by the entrance. He pulled off his helmet and turned at a woman's gasp.

Alanza stared at him with wide eyes. "You're alive! We were all worried something had happened to you."

"Yeah, it took me longer than I expected to make it back. How's Niko? Any change?"

Alanza lowered her gaze. "He's running a fever now and won't eat or drink. Chance doesn't think he'll last more than another day or two." She lifted her head and clasped her hands together. "Were you able to find anything that might help him?"

"No. Everyone was hit hard by the last storm," Leo admitted, tossing his helmet on the rack in frustration. "We're going to have to figure out something else. Let me grab a hydrating pack first and see Skye. Then we can talk about some other options for Niko. Do you know where she is?"

"Um, I'll go grab a hydrating pack for you. You should talk to Daryl," Alanza said and ran toward their supply room.

Leo's eyes narrowed. He tugged off his jacket and dropped it near his helmet, trying to bury the worry that had been plaguing him for the past few days. Something was going on. Otherwise, Skye or Veridian would have come to the entrance when they heard his voice. Alanza should have been pestering him with relentless questions about how they were going to treat Niko instead of running off to fetch him a drink.

Determined to find Skye, he headed down the corridor. Chance intercepted him, his expression one of relief. "Dammit, man. Where the hell have you been?"

"Two of the solar cells on my speeder blew. I had to strip them from my communicator and do a field repair to make it back. It took longer than I expected," Leo said dismissively, glancing down the hall. It was too quiet, and there still wasn't any sign of Skye or Veridian. "What the hell's going on? Where's Skye?"

Chance winced and rubbed the back of his neck. "About that..."

"Where the fuck is she, Chance?"

"A family camp," Daryl said from behind him.

Leo whirled around, the news hitting him like a punch in the gut. He took a step toward Daryl and clenched his fists. "What the fuck are you talking about? If you kicked her out because I was a little late—"

Daryl held up his hand, cutting him off. "You've been gone almost a week, Leo. We had no reason to expect you'd return. I ordered Chance to take the girl to one of the family camps. Skye refused to allow it. It was her decision to go with the kid."

"Of course, she refused!" Leo roared, a dark fury beginning to brew within him. "Kayla would have been exploited or worse. No one would abandon a child there without some sort of guardian. Kayla can't be more than five or six. What the hell were you thinking?"

"I'm not running a fucking charity," Daryl snapped. "Skye had a hard-enough time trying to cover the expenses for her and Veridian. There's no way in hell she'd be able to take care of both kids."

Leo grabbed Daryl and slammed him up against the wall. "You fucking bastard. I more than covered any deficits and you damn well know it. Skye works harder than anyone here. I should kill you for this."

"Leo, don't do this, man," Chance said from behind him. "Let him go."

"And where the hell were *you*, Chance?" Leo demanded.

"I tried to talk her out of it," Chance argued. "That woman was determined to protect those kids, no matter the cost. What the hell did you expect me to do? Skye's got a stubborn streak when it comes to them."

Leo muttered a curse, knowing Chance was right. Skye

rarely listened to him, except when she felt like it. Her passion and conviction were two of the things he loved about her, but it could also be infuriating at times.

Daryl shoved him away, his gaze turning cold. "Don't put this shit on me, Leo. If I make allowances for Skye to take care of two kids, what happens then? When does it stop? If some other woman shows up with a kid, do you expect me to take them in too? What happens if Alanza gets pregnant? Or anyone else? We have these rules for a reason."

"This isn't some random stranger, Daryl. For fuck's sake, Skye's been living in this camp for eight years. You should have given her a chance."

"I did," Daryl said, his tone sharp. "We're out of food, Leo. I'm down five scavengers because of that storm. We're out of medical supplies because you used the last of the metabolic boosters on Skye. I dispatched Jaxon to one of the trading camps with the last of our scavenged items, but all trading has been suspended."

Leo frowned. He'd heard something similar from one of the other scavenging camps he'd visited, but he'd thought it was an isolated event contained to a different district. "You're sure they've all stopped trading? Do you know why?"

"Not a damn clue," Daryl muttered, worriedly running a hand over his head. "No supplies are going out of any trading camps, and they're turning everyone away. In the meantime, I've got more than a dozen people to keep alive without any fucking supplies. I know you care about her, but it's better that Skye's gone. I need people who can mobilize quickly and take the necessary risks. A scavenger with two kids can't outmaneuver a trader crew. They're a liability we can't afford."

Leo crossed his arms over his chest. "This isn't right, Daryl. When Skye came here, she gave you every credit she'd earned working in that trader camp. She's made you thousands more over the years and never refused to do anything you asked of her. Everyone in this camp owes their lives to her in some way, including you. At the first sign of trouble, you throw her back into that hell?"

Daryl blew out a breath. "I'm aware of Skye's value, and I'm sorry to lose her. But running a camp is about making the hard choices, not just the convenient ones. If you intend to lead this camp, you need to learn that. I can't allow her to keep two children here."

Leo was quiet for a long time. "Will you allow her to continue keeping Veridian here?"

Chance straightened. "You found Kayla's camp?"

Leo didn't answer. Instead, he focused on Daryl. "Will you allow Skye to remain here and keep Veridian with her?"

Daryl's gaze turned suspicious. "If she can continue to produce and turn a profit, yes. But I won't make any promises about the future. The girl is out of the question though."

Leo's jaw clenched, and he turned to Chance. "You dropped off Skye?"

Chance nodded. "Two days ago."

"Good. You're coming with me to get them," Leo said, heading back to the exit. He'd hoped for a brief respite after traveling so far, but he wasn't willing to leave Skye and Veridian in one of those camps for a moment longer than necessary. Over his shoulder, he called, "If anything happened to Skye in that camp, Daryl, you'd better not be around when I get back."

CHAPTER NINE

SKYE LEANED FORWARD, adjusting the light near them to better see the wiring she was working on. It wouldn't do any of them much good if she injured herself again. The lack of food, barely drinkable water, and conditions within the camp were already unpleasant enough without adding an injury to the mix. As it was, she was worried about the illness that seemed to be sweeping through the family camp. Despite Tali's assurances, the cough Pete had developed had spread to some of the others. Even Veridian had developed a slight cough earlier that morning, but he was trying to keep it suppressed.

Skye heard Veridian's stomach rumble, and she reached into the bag to pull out one of their few remaining nutrient bars. Breaking it in half, she handed the pieces to the children. Everyone else had gone off to run errands or visit other areas of the camp, so she could risk feeding them without causing an issue. She'd shared a few of her supplies with Tali and the others, but they needed to try to make them last as long as possible. The small plot of land Tali had shown her where they were growing food wasn't large enough to keep everyone sufficiently fed.

Kayla blinked up at her. "You're not hungry?"

Skye gave her a small smile. "I'll eat a bit later. You two need to keep up your strength so you can finish helping me strip that wiring. Afterward, we're going to check the snares we set and help Tali work the garden plot."

Veridian frowned and looked down at his nutrient bar. During the previous night, she'd taken the children out to a nearby scavenging site so they could collect old wiring and other pieces of metal from the ruins. Out here, most of the buildings had already been stripped, but a few things could be found if someone was creative enough.

Veridian and Kayla were in the process of stripping the wiring and brushing the corrosion off the other pieces of metal. Skye had promised to show them how to use the items to create a makeshift battery using old wiring and soil. It wouldn't generate much power, but it was something they could sell within camp or trade for food.

In a quiet voice, Veridian asked, "What do we do when we run out of food?"

"I have a plan," Skye murmured, leaning back against the wall and closing her eyes. "Don't worry about that for now. You two just need to keep looking out for each other."

Skye was so tired. Between keeping watch over the children and making sure their belongings weren't taken, she was exhausted. Walking most of the night to collect supplies hadn't helped either, but she couldn't travel easily during the day with both of them. They didn't have enough UV gear to risk going very far.

The two children were quiet while they nibbled at their food. Skye started to doze until Kayla asked, "Is Leo your dad?"

"Nope," Veridian replied around a mouthful of food. The dry nutrient bar launched another coughing fit, and Skye reached over to hand him some water. He swallowed it and added, "My dad lives in the towers. I want to visit him there when I grow up, but Mom doesn't think they'll let me."

Kayla's eyes widened. She leaned forward and whispered, "There are some bad people living in the towers. You have to stay away from there, or they might hurt you."

Skye frowned, somewhat surprised at the vehemence in Kayla's tone. Some ruin rats felt that way about the towers, so it wasn't altogether surprising. But Skye wasn't willing to risk anyone learning about Veridian's ties to the towers. Other than Leo, she hadn't told anyone else. If someone thought Veridian had some connection to OmniLab, they might try to use him for their own purposes.

"V," she warned.

His face flushed in shame, and he nodded. "I'm not supposed to talk about him. He's gone, and he won't ever come back."

Kayla nodded sagely, her eyes shimmering from unshed tears. "I miss my mom."

Veridian frowned. He was quiet for a long time before he said, "I can share mine with you. Mom stood up for you against Daryl. She does that for me all the time."

Kayla's brow furrowed in confusion. Skye smiled and brushed Kayla's dark hair away from her face. Being alone in the world was a difficult thing, especially for a child.

"Veridian's right," Skye said gently. "I won't ever replace the family you lost, but family comes in all shapes and sizes. Sometimes, the one you choose can be just as important as the one you were born into."

Kayla frowned. "You can choose family?"

Skye reached over to take Kayla and Veridian's hands in

hers. "Trust is a gift. In your life, there are going to be people who want to take advantage of you or hurt you. But there are good people too. The trick is figuring out who's who *before* you get burned."

Kayla cocked her head. "How do you know? Some people pretend to be nice, but they're really not."

"You're right," Skye agreed, wishing she could spare the children from these hard lessons. "You're the only one who can decide who you want to trust. You can't always trust someone's words, but you can trust their actions. It's the choices we make that show who we really are."

Kayla was quiet for a long time. "I heard you talking to Chance. Daryl wanted to send me here by myself, but you wouldn't let him."

Skye sighed. "Daryl's not a bad man, but he's responsible for a lot of people. He made a decision, and I made one too. You're mine to protect, Kayla. You *and* Veridian."

Kayla squared her shoulders, fierce determination shining from her eyes. It was a little disconcerting to see such a thing in a child her age, but Skye knew Kayla would need that steel core to survive. Kayla lifted her head and declared, "I trust you and V."

Skye squeezed Kayla's hand. She might not be able to undo the harm that had been done to Kayla, but it might be possible to soften it. "If you want it, Veridian and I will be your family. From now on, you can always count on us to look out for you. If you're ever not sure about someone, you can trust us. No matter what happens, we look out for each other, yeah?"

Kayla nodded. "Yeah."

Veridian grinned. "Kayla's gonna be my little sister?"

Kayla scowled. "I'm just as big as you."

"But I'm older and know more stuff, like how to fix computers," Veridian said, puffing out his chest a bit.

Kayla frowned. "I can learn that stuff too."

Skye couldn't help but smile. "Yes, and you will. Veridian can teach you, and so will I. There's plenty you can teach both of us too. We all have our strengths. And if you're Veridian's sister, he's your brother. So be good to each other. You two will always be able to rely upon each other."

Veridian looked over at Kayla. "You can trust Leo too. He's going to come get us. Just watch."

Kayla frowned. "Leo helped save me when the building fell."

Skye's heart clenched at the mention of the man she loved. "Yeah. One day, Leo will be camp leader. He'll look after you too. We both will." She squeezed her eyes shut and leaned back against the wall again, hoping her words weren't false hope. If Leo was still alive, he'd make his way here. She had to believe that. But no matter what happened to her or Leo, at least Veridian and Kayla would have each other.

Veridian started coughing again, and Skye frowned. It was getting worse. She offered him the water again, encouraging him to drink. He did and handed the empty canteen back to her. Skye put it down and started rummaging through the bag.

She'd brought the bracelet and coins with her, just in case they needed to make a trade for supplies. Thankfully, she hadn't turned over the items to Daryl. It would be better if she could sell the items directly to a trading camp, since no one here would have the supplies she needed. At the very least, she might be able to buy a ride with one of the coins. She'd need to start making inquiries and find out if Tali could keep an eye on the children for a few hours.

Skye stood and shoved the items into her pocket. "I'm going to get more water. Keep working on the wiring. I'll be back soon. Keep that knife close to you, V."

Both children nodded and went back to their task. Skye

scooped up the canteen and headed outside into the darkness. It was busy with people lingering around, talking or heading to whereabouts unknown. She didn't like leaving the children when there were so many people out, but if Veridian's cough was worsening, he needed to stay hydrated.

The well was situated almost in the center of the camp, which made it a popular meeting spot. They called it a well, but it wasn't exactly that. Large collection tanks had been built to collect rain water and then makeshift pipes had been connected to direct the water over a filter made from small rocks and other sediment. It wasn't as safe or effective compared to the treatment methods used at Daryl's camp, but options were limited. They were fortunate to have this system set up. She'd seen places where people were responsible for their own water collection, using whatever resources they could find.

Skye swept her gaze over the area, making a mental note of possible dangers. A few people were paying her close attention, but no one approached. Satisfied, Skye leaned down to fill the canteen. She felt the air change as though the people around her held their breath. Understanding immediately, she capped off the spigot and straightened.

A man close to his mid-twenties, maybe a handful of years older, walked over to her. His clothing was newer and in better condition than most of the others here. He appeared healthy enough and could easily pass for a scavenger. Most people avoided the family camps, especially if they had another option open to them. It was likely he'd clashed with his camp leader and had been evicted from a scavenging camp relatively recently. At least, that was the best possibility.

Pretending to take her time closing the canteen, Skye held his gaze and waited. If she acknowledged him first, it would mean she wanted something, which she did if he had access to a speeder, but he was the one who'd approached her. She needed to play to whatever advantage she could, even if it was only an illusion.

"The name's Wes."

She inclined her head. "Skye."

He gave her a slow smile, perusing her up and down. "I was asking around about you. No one knows much of anything."

"Nothing to know," she said with a shrug.

"I doubt that," he murmured, assessing her with frank interest. "So tell me, Skye, what camp were you working before you ended up here?"

She arched her brow. "Does it matter?"

"Not overmuch. Call it simple curiosity."

Skye paused, looking him over again. She didn't recognize him, but there were too many scavenging camps to know every ruin rat. Her admission might work either for or against her, but she was desperate enough to take the chance.

"Up until a few days ago, I was with Daryl Markin's camp."

His eyes widened a fraction, and she knew he recognized Daryl's name. It wasn't terribly surprising. Daryl ran one of the larger scavenging camps, but it hadn't always been that way. When she'd found him, Daryl had still been trying to find his way. The credits she'd earned in the trader camp from the previous two years had helped him outfit their camp with gear. From there, they'd been able to establish regular scavenging in higher-risk areas. It had been profitable for everyone involved.

"Impressive. I've heard Daryl can be a bit of a bastard."

She lifted a shoulder in a half-hearted shrug. "Same can be said about most people." Skye took a step toward him, making it obvious she was assessing him in return. "What about you?"

"I was in a smaller camp that usually circulates

throughout the northeast district. Leader was a feisty woman named Malia."

Skye smirked. Based on his cocky demeaner and attitude, she didn't have to make a huge leap to figure out why he wasn't still scavenging there. "Shall I guess why you left?"

Wes barked out a laugh. "You'd probably be right. Malia didn't take too kindly to me after a while, especially when I lost interest in her."

Lifting the canteen, Skye took a drink. "Never a good idea to fuck the camp leader in any sense."

"No shit," he agreed with a grin. "Is that what happened to you?"

"Not even close." Skye paused, cocking her head and studying him. "I'm still wondering why you're here though. A scavenger doesn't usually come back to the family camps without a reason."

"Ah, guess we're done dancing around," Wes said, leaning against the wall. "I've worked two different camps. The first disbanded after the building we were using as a base collapsed. We lost most of our people. I met Malia shortly afterward and joined up with her crew. I was there about a year. After Malia and I parted ways, I decided I'd try striking out on my own."

Skye reached down to top off the canteen again. His story wasn't unusual. It took a special skillset to run a profitable camp. For all Daryl's flaws, he had that talent. But it was still nothing compared to Leo. He not only had the talent but Leo also had the vision to accomplish great things. "So you're here to recruit?"

"And to find people willing to buy in."

She screwed the lid shut on the canteen. "Seems like you're keeping the price low if you're shopping here. Most of these people don't know shit about real scavenging."

"You're here," he pointed out with a smirk. "The way I figure it, you were probably tossed out of Daryl's camp because of those two kids. Don't know your story, but people around here have been talking. It's obvious you and those kids haven't been in a family camp for years. You must have been doing something right."

Skye frowned, considering her options. There weren't many, but Wes probably had transportation. If he was trying to put together a crew, he'd need that and much more. "Not sure what people are saying, but I'm not in a position to buy my way in. As you said, I've got those two kids. They're a handful of years away from going into the ruins."

He studied her for a long time. "Perhaps, but I expect they'll do well once that happens. If they've spent the past several years in a scavenging camp, they've picked up more than most people here."

She arched her brow. "Most people aren't looking ahead a few years if they can't survive the next month."

Wes grinned. "I like to consider myself a visionary."

"I need to get back," she said, starting to turn away. Whatever Wes was peddling was something she couldn't afford to buy. No camp leader in their right mind would take on her and two kids. The fact he was still showing interest didn't sit well with her. Wes might not be a bad guy, but she couldn't afford such a gamble. Not yet anyway.

She'd only made it a couple of steps before Wes called her name.

He jogged up to her. "Skye, wait. I get it. You've got no reason to trust me. But you throw your lot in with mine and we have a chance."

Skye slowed her footsteps but continued walking toward the building where the children were waiting. "You're pitching this awfully hard for someone who knows what sort of baggage I'm carrying. Those kids come first for me. It's why I'm here."

"If they come first, you won't remain here," he said, his tone sharp.

She paused, turning to glare at him. "Talk. Fast."

"You're a scavenger, not just a tech," he said, taking a step closer to her. "I see it in your movements. You marked me the second I approached, probably before. You've got the instincts. If you've been working Daryl's camp for a while, you're good. Better than good. My guess is that storm hit Daryl's camp pretty hard, and he needed to cut someone loose. If you come with two kids, that means you were it. From where I'm standing, you won't stay down on your luck for long. I need your expertise to start up a new camp."

Skye blew out a breath. He'd summed up the situation rather nicely. "How many people do you have committed?"

"Two others. One has experience scavenging. She was cut loose after the last storm too. The other, Mack, is young, but he's eager and hungry to learn. He's done some basic scavenging close to here, but I think he'll do well once we get him in the field."

"Supplies?"

"Ah," Wes murmured and rubbed his chin. "Now that's a bit of a problem. I have a few I've stockpiled, but not enough to get established in the more profitable zones. It'll be night scavenging for a while."

Skye frowned and started walking again. He kept her pace but remained silent while she considered his offer. Night scavenging was dangerous, but she'd done it before. It was common for a new camp starting out until they were able to trade for enough additional supplies. Some camps never made it beyond that point. Sadly, she didn't have many options.

She couldn't remain here, but she was still holding out hope for Leo. Every day that passed, her hope dwindled a little further. It was a tempting thought to go search for Leo herself, but she had no idea where to start or even how. He'd most likely tried to seek out the camps closest to the chasm, but there were hundreds of miles to cover. Dammit. She really needed access to a speeder.

With a sigh, she glanced over at Wes. "You staying here, or making the rounds at family camps?"

"Making the rounds, but I could be persuaded to stay." He waggled his eyebrows and grinned. "Room in your bed for one more?"

Skye snorted. "Yeah, because I need another complication in my life. No, thanks." She darted another glance at him and added, "Your last offer at sharing someone's sleeping mat didn't end too well. You might want to rethink making the same mistake."

"You have a point, but some mistakes are worth it."

Despite herself, Skye's mouth curved upward. Wes was likeable enough, and his offer at starting a new camp was probably the best she was going to get for now. The longer she remained here, the fewer opportunities would come her way.

Stopping outside the building they'd been occupying, Skye said, "I'm not agreeing to join you, but I'll think about it. Circle back around here tomorrow night and I'll let you know."

"Done," he agreed, but they both knew she'd probably accept.

A scream from inside the building interrupted them, and she dashed inside. A man had his arm around Kayla's neck, and Veridian was standing in front of him, wielding the knife. Kayla's eyes were wide and terrified, and Veridian didn't appear to be faring much better. His hand trembled, but he possessed a look of fierce determination.

"Let her go!" Veridian yelled, gripping the knife tightly but not budging from his position in front of the bag.

The man holding Kayla snarled. "Back off, boy. I just want the bag."

Skye narrowed her eyes on Hobb, the man Tali's son had pointed out as a troublemaker the first day they'd arrived. She'd seen him lurking around camp over the past few days, but he'd kept his distance until now. Hobb must have been waiting for her to leave in order to sneak in here. She didn't see a weapon in his hand from this angle, but she wasn't willing to risk it. Even if he was unarmed, it probably wouldn't require much effort to snap Kayla's neck.

"V, move away from him," Skye ordered, making an effort to keep her voice calm when all she wanted was to strangle Hobb. If anything happened to Veridian or Kayla, Hobb wouldn't leave this building alive.

"Listen to your mom," Hobb snapped. "Go stand over there where I can see you."

Veridian tensed. He glanced over at Skye, and she gave him a curt nod. He frowned but did as instructed.

Skye took a small step toward Hobb. "He won't interfere. Release the girl and you can have the bag."

Hobb hesitated, glancing at Wes who was standing behind her. Skye held up her hand to stop Wes from interfering. "Wes, go away. This isn't your concern. We're simply making a friendly trade."

"Not sure it looks too friendly from where I'm standing," he muttered from behind her. "You sure about this?"

"Yes," she said, not taking her eyes off Hobb.

"It's your choice. I'll see you tomorrow."

"Tomorrow," she agreed, listening to Wes's footsteps as he headed outside.

Hobb relaxed slightly. Good. The calmer he was, the more

likely she could get the children out of this situation unharmed.

Skye kept her expression neutral. "I'm not looking for trouble. Release my daughter and take the bag."

"Tell your son to kick over the knife."

Skye stiffened. The last thing she wanted to do was give Hobb a weapon. "It's not enough you're taking our supplies? You want to take our last option for defending ourselves too?"

"Not my problem," Hobb sneered. "Give me the knife and supplies or I'll snap the girl's neck."

Skye turned to Veridian, hoping he'd understand what she was about to say. "V, I know *Chance* showed you how to use that knife and it means a lot to you, but you're gonna need to do what he says. Put it on the ground and kick it over to him."

Veridian stared at her, and she saw understanding dawn in his eyes. Leo had given him the knife and showed him how to use it. Chance had taught him misdirection, and it was that lesson she wanted him to call upon now.

His hand shook as he bent down, placing the knife on the ground. Skye knew he was terrified, but he managed to keep his composure. Angling back, Veridian kicked it a little too hard so it skidded past Hobb and to the far side of the room.

Hobb cursed, and he shoved Kayla in Skye's direction. She grabbed Kayla and pulled her aside just as Wes ran back into the building. He tackled Hobb, falling to the ground and wrestling with him as they both tried to reach the knife. Skye pushed Kayla to safety, and in one fluid movement, withdrew the knife Chance had given her.

Wes was stronger and more powerfully built, but Hobb was desperate. The two of them grappled on the floor, each trying to gain the advantage. Skye couldn't intervene without risking harming Wes. She started to go after Veridian's knife, intending to kick it away, but Hobb's fingers wrapped around it.

"Wes!" she shouted, sliding her weapon on the ground toward him. He grabbed the hilt of the blade just as Hobb sliced across his forearm.

Wes roared loudly, lashing out toward Hobb. The pain and fury must have fueled him because Wes fought like a man possessed. He gripped Skye's knife, slicing outward and cutting Hobb's throat. Blood spurted out, and Skye grabbed the children, trying to avert their eyes. With a garbled cry, Hobb's body went limp.

"Veridian, hurry and grab a couple of old rags from our bag." Skye rushed over to Wes, dropping to her knees beside him. The wound in his arm was deep, cutting through muscle and tendon.

"Fuck, that hurts," Wes muttered.

"No shit." She gripped his arm and turned it to the side to better assess his injury. "It's not pretty either."

Wes grunted an affirmative. "The way I see it, you'll have to join me now. A man takes a hit trying to save you, and the guilt will get you to see reason."

She couldn't help but smile. "You already knew I was probably going to agree."

"Yeah, but I figure you must have other options if you didn't go for it right away. I've never been one for playing those odds when I want something."

Skye blew out a breath and took the rags from Veridian. "Kayla, bring me the canteen."

Kayla picked up the container Skye had dropped when she'd entered the room. She brought it over and asked, "Will he be okay?"

"We're going to make sure of it," Skye said, pouring some of the water over the wound so she could better assess the damage.

Wes hissed in pain. Between gritted teeth, he said, "Cute kid."

Skye made a noise of agreement. "It's a deep wound. Tell me you have some medical supplies in your stockpile."

"No such luck."

Skye frowned. She still had the bracelet she'd acquired a few days ago. It had been her hope to wait to trade it when things became dire, but things were looking that way already. The fact Wes had stepped in to help her had established a level of debt between them—Skye *always* paid her debts.

"I can wrap it temporarily, but you're going to need more than what we have here if you want to keep the use of that arm. I may have something to trade for additional supplies, but I'll need a ride to a trading camp."

Wes arched a brow. "Only ten minutes with me and you've already changed my luck."

Skye smiled. "Kayla, come here and hold the cloth in place. Veridian, grab another cloth. I'll show you how to field dress a wound."

The children gathered beside her as she showed them how to bandage the injury. Veridian had seen it done several times before, but Kayla watched with wide eyes. She asked several questions, displaying an intelligence that was surprisingly adult in nature. When she finished, Skye picked up both knives and handed one of them back to Veridian. She poured some of the water over her hands to clean off the blood and then did the same to Kayla's hands. "We're going to have to get you a weapon soon."

"Will you show me how to use it?"

Skye made a noise of agreement. "Sure thing."

"Leo showed me how to use mine. I bet he can show you too," Veridian volunteered, tucking his knife into his waistband.

A sharp pang of sadness rushed through Skye at the

thought of Leo again. Once she left the family camp and accepted Wes's offer, it was unlikely she'd see him again. Ruin rats moved around too much to keep track of each other for long. She could try to get a message to Chance, but if Leo was around to receive it, he would have come for them already.

A lump formed in her throat. Leo was gone, and the thought of a life without him in it was more painful than she'd ever imagined. She could try to wait another day or two and hope he'd show, but she was responsible for two other lives now. They needed to come first, even if it destroyed part of her to give up on Leo.

She studied Veridian and Kayla, who looked up at her with eyes full of trust. Regret and grief would need to come later—once she'd ensured their safety. These two children were the future, and she had a responsibility to make sure they survived—even if her heart didn't.

———

LEO CLIMBED OFF THE SPEEDER, motioning for Chance to keep an eye on both vehicles. He wouldn't put it past anyone in the family camp to relieve them of their expensive equipment. While he didn't begrudge anyone their right to survival, he wasn't about to relinquish his.

The familiar sound of the camp's UV-protective shield was reassuring. Some of the family camps didn't even have that luxury. His boots crunched over the well-worn path, and he swept his gaze over the area. He was attracting attention, which was what he expected, but no one had yet approached him. Family camps tended to be more welcoming to women and children, which might explain some of their reservations. He only hoped Skye had been greeted more warmly.

Pausing near one of the small groups of people, he

focused on one of the older women. "I'm looking for a woman. Blonde. Blue eyes. She would have arrived last week."

"Lots of people come through here," the woman said, eyeing him up and down as though taking his measure. When she tensed and took a half-step backward, he understood her reservations. She'd either marked him as a member of a scavenging camp or willing to take what he wanted from those who were weaker. Either way, she obviously didn't trust his intentions.

He decided to try again. "She goes by the name of Skye. Two kids—a boy and a girl—would have been with her."

The woman pursed her lips and shrugged. "Maybe I've seen her. Maybe I haven't. If so, what would you be wanting with her?"

Leo took a step toward the older woman. "If you're protecting her, I mean her no harm. She's mine. I need to get a message to her."

Another younger woman standing nearby cocked her head. "What's your name?"

"Leo," he said, hoping these women knew something.

The two women exchanged a look. He barely resisted the urge to demand they take him to Skye. The only thing that stopped him was the understanding they were trying to protect her.

Leo looked around at the buildings and at the people lingering nearby. If he even tried to enter or search them one by one, more than a few members of the camp would likely attack him. None of these people knew him or had reason to trust him.

Reaching into his bag, he pulled out a nutrient bar. He held it out and said, "It's yours if you'll take a message to her and let her know I'm looking for her."

The older woman stared at the nutrient bar. After a long

moment, she gave him a curt nod and took the food. "Wait here."

He watched as the woman motioned to a young man standing close to them. She whispered something in his ear and the boy took off to whereabouts unknown.

———

GRYPH CAME RUNNING into the room from a back entrance, skidding to an abrupt halt at the sight of Hobb dead on the ground. "You killed him?"

Skye lifted her head and frowned. "I'm glad you're back, Gryph. We're going to need some help dragging Hobb out of here. Do you know where they dispose of the bodies?"

Gryph swallowed and nodded. "Yeah. It's just outside of camp. I can round up some people to drag him out of here, but there's a man here to see you. Tali wanted me to let you know. He looks like he's from a scavenging camp."

"It's probably Chance," Veridian said, glancing toward the door. "Want me to bring him here for you, Mom?"

"Yeah. Chance said he'd drop off supplies in a few days," she said, turning back to Wes who appeared to be in a significant amount of pain. "Kayla, why don't you go with V? Stay together."

Kayla nodded, and the three children ran outside together. At least with Hobb dead, one potential problem was resolved. Chance wouldn't let anything happen to them, and it was just a short distance to the outside of the camp.

"Cute kids," Wes muttered, studying his bandaged arm. "We can make arrangements to head out of here tonight, if you're up for it. I've been scouting some possible locations that might be suitable. We can walk through the night and hole up there during the day until we move on."

Skye sat back on her heels. "If Chance is here, he may

have brought a transport vehicle. He can take us where we want to go. Do you have a temporary camp set up?"

"Not yet," Wes said and then muttered a curse as he moved his injured arm. "Driving may be somewhat challenging right now. I don't mind taking your friend up on any offer he's willing to make if it'll help get us deeper into OmniLab territory."

Skye frowned. "Keep that arm still. Once we get to the new camp location, we can look into trading for something to treat that."

"You won't hear me arguing," Wes muttered. "That new scavenger I mentioned, Mack, is here and eager to get started. I'll have him help move out the body. We can take off right after that. Fuck, this hurts."

Skye nodded and walked over to her bag. She started rolling up their sleeping mats and shoved them into the bag. At least with Chance's arrival, she could get a message to Leo about where she'd gone. If she was honest with herself, Leo was the main reason she hadn't taken Wes up on his offer right away.

Wes crouched beside her. "You're making the right decision."

Skye arched an eyebrow. "Did I give you the impression I had doubts?"

"No, but you're a little hard to read. You've got guts. Taking on this guy who was threatening your kids shows me I was right about you. I want this to work, Skye. I think you need me just as much as I need you."

She made a noncommittal noise and closed the bag. "Then let me start out this relationship by making a few things clear. To begin with, I have no intention of sleeping with you."

His mouth curved upward. "Noted, but I'll remain hopeful."

She couldn't help but smile. "Second, those two kids come first for me. I won't put them in jeopardy. If I believe there's a danger to them from any source, I'm gone. I know you're just starting out, but I won't stay in a camp with anyone who might be a threat to them."

Wes studied her for a long time. "I'll make you a deal."

"What?"

He leaned toward her. "You stick with me, and you have final say in who stays and goes. *You* decide who we recruit and I'll go along with it." When she arched her brow, he grinned and added, "I told you, I want this to work."

Skye's smile deepened, and she shook her head in exasperation. "You reek of desperation, Wes. We need to talk about your negotiation skills if you plan on handling traders."

He chuckled. "That's exactly why I need you."

"Why do I have the feeling you really don't want to run your own camp?"

"Perceptive too," he said with a grin.

She tilted her head. "Then why are you doing this?"

Wes sighed and ran a hand over his head. "I was honest with you before. I'm tired of bouncing from camp to camp. I want something more permanent. The only way to get that, at least in part, is to run my own crew. A lot of these camps don't seem to last long. They're mismanaged."

Skye frowned. "I've never run a camp. I've always worked for other people."

He shrugged. "Then we're in the same situation. Between the two of us, maybe we can figure out the rest."

Skye lowered her gaze and stared at her packed bag. Leo would know. He had the expertise to start his own camp, but she wasn't sure if he was ready to take that step yet. But first, she needed to find him. Lifting her head, she said, "I'll do what I can for you, but once Chance takes us to a new camp location, I want a favor."

"What's that?"

"I'll need to use your speeder for a day. There's someone who went missing right before I left Daryl's camp. I need to reach out to a couple of nearby scavenging camps to find out if they've seen him."

He frowned. "If you find him, will it change your mind about joining me?"

"It might," she admitted, not wanting to say anything that might jeopardize his agreement. But she needed to be honest with him.

"Damn," he muttered. "I'm guessing he's also the reason you're determined not to sleep with me too."

Skye smiled and didn't respond.

Wes sighed. "Yeah. We can get word to some nearby camps. At least once you reach out to them, I'll know you're committed."

"Thanks, Wes," she said and kissed his cheek. "I'll do whatever I can for you."

Footsteps sounded from outside, and she glanced up just as someone entered.

"Leo," Skye managed on a whisper and pushed up off the ground. The sight of the man she loved beyond all reason standing in front of her was something she wasn't sure she'd ever see again. He murmured her name, and she launched herself at him. Wrapping her arms around his neck, she laid her head against his chest. Tears streaked down her cheeks as she held on to him. "You're alive! I can't believe you're here. I was so scared I'd lost you."

Leo gripped her tightly, burying his face in her hair. "Baby, I'm so sorry. My speeder broke down, and I couldn't get back to you soon enough. Chance is outside keeping an eye on the kids."

She curled her fingers into the material of his jacket, unwilling to let him go. The uncertainty of the last several days crashed into her, and along with it, all the emotions she'd been suppressing. If she was dreaming, she never wanted to wake up.

Wes cleared his throat. She wiped away her tears and turned to look at him. He grinned and said, "Let me guess... he must be the reason you wanted to use my speeder?"

She smiled and nodded. Leo wrapped his arm around her waist and frowned at Hobb's dead body on the ground. "What the hell happened? Are you okay? Did he hurt you?"

Skye shook her head. "I'm fine. Promise." She gestured to Wes. "Leo, this is Wes. We ran into some problems and he helped us. That's how he got hurt."

Leo frowned and held out his hand to Wes. "In that case, I owe you a debt."

"I'm really glad to hear you say that," Wes said, reaching out to shake Leo's hand. "I have a proposition for both of you."

Leo narrowed his eyes. "What?"

Skye smiled and leaned against Leo. He was naturally suspicious and rightfully so. Pressing her hand against his chest, she said, "Wes is starting his own camp. He was trying to recruit me."

"Skye already has a camp," Leo said with a frown.

"From where I'm standing, it doesn't look that way," Wes reminded him. "Don't know you or your situation, but I know Skye's been here alone with those kids for almost a week. Any loyalty for Daryl died right about the time he dropped her off in this camp."

"Daryl made a mistake," Leo said, his tone a little sharper than necessary. "She's coming back with me."

"Is she?" Wes asked, crossing his arms over his chest. "What happens if you're delayed again? You gonna take the chance she ends up back here? I can offer her something more."

Leo released her and took a threatening step toward Wes. "If you want to have a problem with me, keep talking. I'm not about to let Skye go with some asshole she met a few days ago."

"Leo," Skye said quietly and put her hand on his arm.

Leo spun around and glared at her. "You can't be serious. What do you know about this guy? He helps you out and you're ready to walk away? Just like that?"

Wes cleared his throat. "I'll give you two some time to talk. I'll be right outside."

Skye waited until he was gone, and then turned back to Leo.

"Fuck that, Skye. I'm not letting you go. I don't know what he promised you—"

"Is that what you think?" she demanded, taking a step toward him. She jabbed her finger against his chest and added, "Do you really think I would walk away from you? You're the only man I want—the man I love! I'm not letting you go either, you stubborn idio—"

Leo hauled her against him and kissed her, silencing her more completely than any argument he could have made. Skye closed her eyes, getting lost in the taste and feeling of him. This was the man who meant everything to her. She'd always struggled with knowing who to trust, but Leo had always been the exception. In every way that counted, he'd always looked out for her. He was her salvation and her hope for the future. The gruff and abrasive exterior was simply a mask designed to protect himself from the harshness of the world. But with her, she saw the real Leo—the man he kept hidden from the rest of the world—and he was more wonderful than anyone she'd ever known.

He broke their kiss and pressed his forehead against hers. "I don't know what I'd do if I lost you, Skye. Sometimes, I think you're the only thing good in this world. I was ready to kill Daryl when I heard he'd forced you out."

Skye swallowed, her earlier irritation evaporating at the vulnerability in his eyes. "Wes isn't wrong, Leo. I can't take Veridian and Kayla back to Daryl's camp. He won't let me keep both of them, and I won't give her up. I can't. I made her a promise."

"Shit," he muttered and then sighed. "I didn't have any luck finding Kayla's camp. What do you want to do?"

Skye lowered her gaze and ran her hands over his jacket. Part of her had known Daryl wouldn't let her return with Kayla, but it only reaffirmed her decision. "I don't trust Daryl anymore. I'm not sure I ever did, but coming here made me realize I need to follow a leader I respect."

"What are you saying?"

Skye looked up at him. "I'd follow *you*, Leo."

Leo's eyes widened. "You want me to take over Daryl's camp?"

She nodded. "If you don't want to take over Daryl's camp, then I want to start over somewhere else with you. But I owe Wes for what he did for me just now. He wants to start a new camp, but he doesn't want to run it. This could be an opportunity for us."

Leo frowned. "Daryl's camp will fall apart if we leave, and he's not ready to step aside yet."

"I know," Skye whispered, thinking about everyone in Daryl's camp that she cared about. She didn't want to lose them, but they were all adults who could fend for themselves. Veridian and Kayla needed her; they were her priority. "This has to be your decision, Leo."

He sighed. "Tell me about Wes."

"I only just met him, but I need to try to get him some medical attention. The only reason he was injured was to protect us. I told him I had some items I could use to trade for medical supplies at an Omni trading camp."

Leo's frown deepened. "The trading camps are shut down."

"What?"

"I don't know what's going on, but they've suspended trading," Leo said, running a hand over his short hair. "I heard rumors from some of the camps I visited. There's a problem of some kind at the towers and they've recalled the traders. Daryl's in a panic over it, and Alanza's hysterical because it's almost certain Niko won't survive another day."

"There has to be a way to get some supplies," Skye whispered, trying to quell her worry. Too many people would suffer if they weren't able to trade with the Omnis. "Without them, we're out of options."

Leo was quiet for a long time. "I might have a solution, but it'll be risky."

"What?"

Leo took a step closer to her. "You know the layout of the southeast trading camp. Do you still remember their security setup?"

She jerked her head up. "What are you thinking?"

"I need you to trust me, baby," he said, brushing his thumb across her cheek. "The trading camps may be shut down, but you know the access codes and how their system works. We can still get those supplies, just not by trading for them."

Skye stared at him in shock. "They would have changed the codes. It's been years, Leo."

"We can hack into it," he said, taking her hands in his. "We don't have a choice. I'm not going to lose you. If you want to keep both kids with us, we need to make our offer to Daryl extremely attractive. If we hit a trader camp, Daryl won't have a choice. And if not, fuck him. We'll start over again... with each other."

Skye frowned, glancing toward the door where Wes was waiting. Leo wouldn't propose something so dangerous unless he truly believed it was their best option. If they failed in this, they'd lose everything—including their lives. Above all else, she trusted Leo.

Turning back to him, she nodded. "Wes needs supplies too. Let's get Hobb's body out of here, and then we can make plans. I'm not willing to lose you either."

CHAPTER TEN

SKYE WORKED on mapping out the layout of the trading camp while Leo set up the on-board console on the cargo vehicle for Veridian and Kayla. Wes had eagerly agreed to Leo's plan, intent on trying to acquire as many of the supplies he'd need to get his camp off the ground. The young scavenger Wes had brought along had proven to be eager and competent so far, but they'd see how he handled being in the field. After all, Mack was only a handful of years older than Veridian.

Chance had agreed to keep an eye on Mack, but the more people they had to help, the better their luck might hold. They'd each need to play a vital part to accomplish their goals. Part of her couldn't believe they were actually considering such a bold move against OmniLab, but their plan was daring enough that it might just work. At least, she hoped.

Skye considered the design and made a few small changes to bring it more to scale. It had been eight years since she'd worked in Tyler's trading camp. Even if they made some changes during that time, it was unlikely they'd completely revamped their protocol or even the camp setup.

Wes leaned over her shoulder and pointed to an area on the diagram. "What's that room?"

"Crew's quarters," she said, modifying the design to account for different variables. "They set up individual areas based on the number of people working in the camp. It can hold up to thirty people, but it's not usually that full. We can avoid that area completely, provided we get access to the main control center."

"And if we can't?"

She blew out a breath. "Then we're screwed. There's no way to know how many people are still there. We need to lock it down, and that requires access to the control center. Even if they recalled the traders to the towers, I don't think everyone would have gone." She paused, considering the diagram for a long time. "OmniLab never did a recall while I was there. I just can't imagine them taking a bunch of ruin rats to the towers. A few of us went to the towers to pick up supplies, but we weren't even allowed in the front door. They took us to a holding area in the garage where they transferred pallets to our vehicles."

Wes smirked. "I knew your expertise would come in handy. I just didn't realize how much."

She smiled. "Yeah. If we survive this, I'll accept the compliment. Until then, don't jinx it."

Leo booted up the system and configured it to sync with their comms. "And we're live. Chance, where are we with the transport?"

"It's all checked out, boss," Chance replied with a mock salute. "The engine power's been boosted. Mack's got a good eye for mechanical work. We're good to go."

"Don't call me 'boss.'" Leo grabbed the canteen and took a drink.

Skye grinned. "I don't know. I kinda like the sound of that. It's pretty hot."

Leo arched his brow. "*You* can call me that. I'll kick Chance's ass if he calls me that again."

She laughed and pushed the map toward Leo. "This is about as accurate as it's going to get. Everyone going inside needs to memorize the layout."

Mack walked over and studied the diagram. He was barely thirteen, but ruin rats had to grow up quickly. Unfortunately, he was still in that phase where he was convinced he was invincible. This whole thing was one big adventure to him.

"You really worked for those assholes, huh?"

Skye didn't answer Mack right away. Instead, she glanced over at her son who watched the conversation with curiosity. She'd only told him a few things about his father. Once he was older, she planned to share more, but it was hard enough for Veridian knowing his father lived in the towers and they'd never have a chance to meet.

"Not all traders are bad. The trader I worked with was fair. His replacement was something of a bastard though. You can't judge them all based on the same cutout."

Wes made a noncommittal noise. "So what's the plan? How are we going to approach their camp?"

"That's going to be a little tricky," Skye admitted, pulling up the diagram showing the outside area. "They have ground sensors circling about a two-mile radius from the camp. It's set to pick up any transportation units, so we'll have to go on foot."

Chance gaped at her. "You want to try walking it? The sun's going to be up in another couple of hours. If something goes wrong or we don't make it out of there in time, we're screwed."

"There's no 'we' in this scenario," Leo said, leaning over the diagram. "Skye and I will be the ones to walk it. You, Wes, and Mack need to wait here with the cargo vehicle until we send a signal. Veridian and Kayla will remain here as well.

Too many people on the initial approach will increase our chances of being caught."

Wes frowned. "The trading camp will pick up the signal from the cargo vehicle the minute we cross the perimeter."

Skye nodded. "We should be able to get you the frequencies to mask your signal. You'll just need to sit tight until we get through the perimeter and into their camp."

Chance rubbed his chin thoughtfully. "I'm not particularly fond of sitting on the sidelines, but it sounds like that's our best option."

Leo frowned, studying the diagrams showing the outside and interior of the camp. "They have cameras when we get closer. Can we avoid those?"

Skye sighed. The cameras were going to be a problem. "We're going to try. I've routed a path we can take to avoid the outlying cameras based on where they used to be located. There were a few holes in their security back then, but it's been years since I last worked inside the camp. It's going to be a risk."

Kayla peeked over her shoulder. "Electricity hums. Can't you listen for it?"

Skye frowned and glanced down at her. "What do you mean, sweetheart?"

"Are we really going to listen to a kid?" Mack asked with a scowl. "She doesn't know what she's talking about. You can't hear cameras."

"Hey, don't talk to her like that." Veridian stood and moved beside Kayla in a show of solidarity. Leo started to step forward to intervene, but Skye shook her head in warning and held up her hand to stop him. Leo frowned at her but remained silent, his expression mildly curious.

If Veridian and Kayla were going to work together, they needed to cement their bond now. They'd need to depend upon each other if things went bad in the future. She wanted them to have something like what she'd found in Leo. There wasn't anyone she trusted more, and no one should have to be alone in this world.

Kayla glared at Mack and put her hands on her hips. "You're a kid too. And I know what I'm talking about."

"Like hell," Mack muttered, crossing his arms over his chest, but he didn't argue further. It was enough. Mack might be irritated with Kayla, but he wouldn't take on both children. Leo arched an eyebrow, and Skye smiled. She'd have to explain everything to him later.

Focusing on Kayla again, Skye kept her voice gentle as she asked, "Can you tell me what you meant about a hum?"

Kayla hesitated, her shoulders relaxing now that Mack had backed off. "Electricity and equipment make noise. The family camp was really quiet when they shut off the UV guard. I thought maybe you could hear the cameras too."

Skye's eyes widened at the implication. "She's right. If we can configure a commlink to listen for the frequencies being used by the cameras, we might be able to identify any holes in their security. But even if we can't hear them, we may be able to jam the signal at least to slip through. We can also use the same tactic on the cameras mounted to the building."

"Well, I'll be damned. The kid might have a point," Chance said, reaching over to grab a commlink. "It'll just take me a minute so you can read the signals."

Skye beamed a smile at Kayla. "Well done. You'll be an expert in no time."

Kayla straightened at the praise, and Veridian bumped shoulders with her. He leaned in close and whispered loudly, "We're gonna be the best scavenging team ever."

Leo made a noise of agreement. "Let's see about making it through today first. We'll work on the scavenging bit later. Veridian and Kayla, you're going to stay on the transport with Chance."

Veridian frowned. "I can help."

Kayla nodded. "We both want to help."

Skye smiled at them. "Good. That's exactly what we need. You're going to have a very important job."

Kayla and Veridian exchanged a determined look between them. Skye bit back a smile and motioned them over to the console Leo had configured. "We need you to monitor the radar. If anyone appears on it, I need you to let us know right away so we can hide. But it's very important that you don't speak over our communication devices unless there's an emergency."

Veridian nodded solemnly. "We won't."

"Can't you use a different channel so you can talk?" Kayla asked with a frown, staring at the screen. "They can't check all of them."

Skye smiled and ran a hand over Kayla's hair. Kayla was a little too clever. She'd frustrate the hell out of the traders when she got older. "You're right, but they automatically scan them for chatter. If they hear us, they'll focus on us to see why we're in the vicinity. We need to keep a low-profile. Maybe one day we should think about using code words. Why don't you and Veridian start coming up with some you can use when you start scavenging together?"

Kayla nodded and leaned in to look at the code Leo had put on the screen. Veridian started pointing things out to her and telling her what they meant.

Skye glanced over at Leo to see his brow creased with concern. Unlike the children, they both knew if anything went wrong, there was no coming back from it. Being black-listed from all OmniLab trading districts was the best scenario. At the worst, they'd be executed and the children would be on their own. She turned to look at Veridian again, knowing it was a real possibility she wouldn't be able to watch him grow up.

Chance put his hand on Skye's shoulder and squeezed it gently before handing her the commlink. "They'll be okay. I'll look out for them. You just focus on what needs to be done."

Veridian met her gaze. "Mom, we've got this."

"Right," she agreed, forcing herself to turn away. If she hesitated any longer, they might lose their window of opportunity. Most trading camps kept to a set shift schedule. They should be changing shifts in another few hours. The goal was to get inside while people were tired and not as alert and before the next shift woke up. They'd still meet opposition, but they might be able to get in and out to minimize the potential loss of life.

It didn't sit right with her at the thought of possibly harming those who worked in the trading camp. Some of them might have been her co-workers at one time. If their situation wasn't quite so desperate, Skye never would have agreed to this.

Leo motioned her over to the speeder. She nodded and followed him. Everyone else would wait outside the perimeter while they attempted to disable the surveillance. The cargo vehicle Chance was driving had been temporarily retrofitted to boost the speed with the engines from two of their other speeders. It was the only way they could manage to take everyone on one vehicle and still be able to transport any supplies they acquired.

Skye climbed on, scooting forward so Leo could get on behind her. She knew of a nearby ruin just outside the surveillance perimeter where they could hide the speeder. Pulling away from the other vehicles, she headed back toward the Omni trading camp and the memories that went along with it.

———

"THAT SHOULD BE the last of the outlying cameras," Skye whispered to Leo.

They were crouched near a boulder not far from the trading camp. From this position, she could see the storage area entrance where the Omni trading camp kept their vehicles. Once they crossed the threshold, they'd be entering the point of no return.

She glanced over at Leo. "Are you sure you want to do this?"

"We need those supplies. I'm not risking losing you again," Leo said quietly, studying the trading camp. "I can make it the rest of the way on my own. Why don't you go ahead and turn back? I'll give the signal when it's safe."

She shook her head and put her hand over his. "We're partners. I'm not going to risk losing you either. If we're doing this, we go in together."

Leo turned toward her and cupped her face. "Those kids need you, Skye. Let me do this for you."

She swallowed and looked up into his eyes. It was just like him to try to take on the world to protect her. "They need both of us, Leo, and *I* need you. Our chances are better if I go in with you. If there's anyone I used to know, they might listen to me. I'm not letting you walk in there without me."

He searched her expression for a long time before sighing. "You're an incredibly stubborn woman."

She couldn't help but smile. "You're equally as stubborn."

"Those fucking dimples of yours," he muttered with a trace of a smile. "I can't say no to you. Come on."

Her smile deepened, and she got up from her crouch and scrambled over the rock to move closer to the camp with Leo following behind her.

Most ruin rats lived in temporary camps or abandoned buildings, but the Omni traders used more permanent establishments as their base of operations. There were four trading camps in total, and the areas around the Omni towers were divided into different districts. Each trader oversaw operations being conducted within their particular district.

The vehicle storage room was a covered area that led directly into the camp. There were only two entrances into the trading camp, the main one and the emergency exit. With the emergency exit being completely sealed off except from the inside, their only option was to walk through the front door.

Skye stopped right outside the storage area and put her hand on Leo's arm in warning. He froze, waiting for her signal. She studied the floor of the garage and then focused on the walls. In the right light, you could see the normally invisible detection beams as they moved up and down. They needed to hurry, but timing was going to be everything. Once she spotted them, she motioned toward the beams and mimicked their sweeping movements with her hand. Leo nodded, indicating he saw the beams too.

"Now," she whispered and darted forward. They dove to the floor to miss the security beams and crawled the rest of the way into the garage. No alarms. With her heart pounding in her chest, Skye got to her feet and moved silently toward the far wall.

Leo crouched down beside one of the speeders and began removing the cover to the onboard computer system. While he was working on trying to obtain the codes to send to Chance, she scanned the length of the garage. The number of speeders and vehicles was less than what she'd expected. It was likely only ten people remained within the camp. At least half of them would be sleeping, while the rest would be winding down and looking forward to getting off shift.

Unlike some of the ruin rat camps, the trading camps primarily scavenged during the daytime. But they always had at least a few people working around the clock on various projects. In addition to scavenging, the trading camps were just that—focused on trading for artifacts with the ruin rats. Each artifact they obtained had to be assessed, catalogued, and then carefully packaged before being sent to the towers. Every week, supplies had to be picked up from the towers, inventoried, and then stored in preparation for trading with the ruin rats.

Depending on how long trading had been shut down, their inventory may be sparse. They'd still have some in reserve, and Skye knew where the excess was probably stored. But it wouldn't be as large of a haul as if they'd just picked up a new shipment from the towers.

"Got it," Leo whispered, reattaching the cover. "I just sent Chance the frequency codes to mask his signal on approach. You ready to move in to disable the surveillance?"

She nodded. "See if you can find something to use for the door."

Keeping her footsteps silent, she moved toward the main entrance. Once upon a time, access had been as simple as putting her hand on the console serving as an electronic door lock. Unfortunately, brute force was the only way to gain entry now. Leo handed her the tool, and she pried off the cover. They couldn't override the electronic lock this way, but she could disable the alarms while they manually pried it open.

She put the cover on the floor and held up a light to study the wiring. Not everyone who worked in the trading camp knew all the security features, and she wasn't an exception. But her relationship with Tyler had given her some additional insights. He'd trusted her, and she'd walked in on a few conversations he'd had with other crew members. Over time, she'd managed to piece together a better idea of how everything worked.

The wiring was all color coded, but there were enough

decoys to make it nearly impossible for anyone to circumvent it. Pulling out her multi-purpose tool, Skye located what appeared to be two ground wires. Only one of them was used for that function, but the other was the line for the alarm system. She quickly cut both of them. Severing the real ground wire wouldn't alert anyone unless they happened to be running a diagnostic on the system at that moment, and they could repair the safety wire easily enough.

"We're good," she said, motioning for Leo to help her with the door.

He bent down and shoved the edge of a piece of metal into the door. Using it as a lever, he forced open the door a fraction. She shoved her fingers into the crevice and he did the same. Using their combined strength, they pulled the door open enough to slip inside.

The moment they entered, the springs on the door sealed it shut behind them. Skye took a steadying breath and crept along the wall. Silence was their only friend now.

The control room was located on the far side of the camp. They could either head through the main common area or directly through the crew's quarters. Even though people would be sleeping in the crew's quarters, the common area was riskier.

She passed by what once had been Tyler's office. The door was closed, which wasn't surprising since the trader currently assigned to this post was probably back at the towers. She started to move farther down the hallway, but approaching footsteps made her halt.

"Yeah, but I thought I heard something," someone said from an adjacent room.

Leo pushed open the door to Tyler's office, and she darted inside with him. He closed the door quietly behind them and leaned against the wall to wait. She glanced over at him in the dim lighting. That was a little too close. He pressed his ear against the door, but she tapped his arm and shook her head.

Motioning for him to follow, she crossed the room and pressed a small button hidden on the far wall. A panel slid open, leading directly to the trader's private quarters. She closed the door behind him and let out the breath she'd been holding.

"We can talk in here," she said, pulling out a light to see how much had changed. The few personal possessions Tyler had kept in here were long gone. They'd gone through at least two other traders since then. She didn't know this new one, but they never lasted longer than five years. OmniLab didn't keep them in the field longer than that.

"This room isn't monitored?"

She shook her head. "No. It's also soundproofed. The privacy screens in the office weren't activated, so anyone walking by could have heard us. The power draw is too high to keep them engaged when they're not needed. But the noise-insulating effect in here is built into the walls."

Leo frowned and gazed around the room. "This is the trader's quarters, isn't it? Won't they look for us in here?"

Skye shook her head, trailing her fingertips over one of the shelves of the wall unit. Several artifacts were on display, most likely prized possessions belonging to the trader. "No. Except for the crew, no one knows about the secondary entrance through the office. The main one is through the hallway, but it's usually kept locked." She opened the locker to look inside at the neatly folded clothing. "It's unlikely the new trader changed that, especially with his personal items here. We're safe enough at the moment."

She paused at the bed and then forced herself to look away. There were too many memories here. She'd once been happy in this place, before it had robbed her of so much.

"Hey," Leo began, moving to stand next to her. He turned

her around to look at him and tilted up her chin. "He was an idiot for letting you go. I'm not going to do the same."

She managed a smile and kissed him lightly. "If I'd met you first, I never would have looked twice at him."

He searched her expression. "It's hard being here, isn't it?"

"Yes, but not for the reasons you're probably thinking," she admitted and looked around the room once more. "I want Veridian to have a future, Leo. It scares me to think he's going to spend the rest of his life struggling while his father's living in the safety of the towers."

"He has you, Skye. That's more than he would have living there. You're the best mother I've ever known, and Veridian's lucky to have you."

Skye swallowed. "There's something I want to ask you. I know I don't have any right, but..." Her voice trailed off as she looked away.

"You can ask me anything. What is it?"

"Being here, in this place again... I know Veridian isn't your responsibility, but he looks up to you, Leo. If something does happen to me or I don't make it out, will you look out for him?"

"Hey," Leo said gently, lifting her chin again to look into her eyes. "Nothing's going to happen to you. But you have my word. I'll always protect him the same way I'd protect you. I love him too, Skye. I love both of you."

Her eyes welled with tears, and she threw her arms around his neck. Leo had always been a man of his word. If he made a promise, he held to it. She buried her face against his chest, love nearly overwhelming her.

Leo wrapped his arms around her, pulling her close. "We're going to make it out of here fine, baby. You'll see."

She nodded. Running her hands down his chest, she said, "I know. Sometimes, I think you can do just about anything."

"With you by my side, absolutely. Come on. I'm sure

they're gone by now. We need to get in and back out before the sun comes up."

Taking a steadying breath, she pulled away from him and led him back into the trader's office. They approached the door, and Leo listened against it. In a quiet voice, he said, "It's clear."

She opened the door, and they slipped back out into the hallway. Staying close to the wall, she crept forward until she could see around the corner. It was clear.

The crew's quarters were located in one large room, divided up into small, private quarters. Electronic privacy dividers were set up, sectioning off each mini room. She still remembered the first time she'd seen such opulence and how much it had astounded her. In all honesty, it was one of the things she missed most about the trader camp.

A small red light shone outside some of the private areas, indicating the residents were inside and didn't want to be disturbed. Skye counted them quickly. As she expected, five people were currently sleeping, which meant no more than five would be awake. That was still more than she wanted to deal with, but their odds had just increased dramatically.

She led Leo through the crew's quarters to another hallway. The soft sound of voices could be heard farther down the hall, somewhere in the vicinity of the tech room or communication room. The easiest and fastest way to disable the surveillance would be from the tech room, but that wasn't going to be an option. They'd definitely be spotted, and they needed to keep this operation as quiet as possible. Instead, Skye headed the opposite direction toward the maintenance room.

Leo closed the door behind them, and Skye tapped her lips with her finger, indicating the need to be quiet. This room wasn't soundproofed. Leo nodded and began investigating some of the equipment being stored in here while she activated the terminal in the corner of the room.

Skye readily admitted she wasn't the best tech. It had never interested her overly much. She'd always preferred the glamour and excitement of scavenging in long-abandoned ruins. But she knew more about this particular camp than Leo, so this next part would be up to her.

Taking a deep breath, she pulled up the file mapping for the entire camp. Tyler's old administrative password would have been changed years ago, but there had to be a way to access the surveillance system from the backend. They would still need to be able to access some of the systems in the event of an emergency or if the trader was off-site.

Leo leaned over her shoulder to look at the screen while she scanned through the different folders. It was more disorganized than she expected. Things were mislabeled or filed incorrectly. It was a wonder how they managed to keep this camp profitable.

Leo pointed to a folder on the screen and whispered close to her ear, "What's that?"

She frowned and opened up the file folder. Dozens of internal memos appeared on the screen, along with some rather strange headings. She opened one of the most recent memos and began reading. Her eyes widened at the information.

The leader of the Omni Towers had died in some sort of accident, along with a dozen other members of something called the Inner Circle. Skye didn't know much about their hierarchy in the towers, but her thoughts drifted back to the conversation she'd had with Tyler about a circle. This must be the same circle he'd spoken of with such fear. If these were important people, it made sense that all the traders and other Omni personnel had been recalled immediately to the towers.

She flipped through to the next memo. It contained more

details about the status of the trading camps. Trading was suspended until they restored order to their government and an investigation was concluded. Skye frowned, more determined than ever to confiscate the supplies they needed. OmniLab would ensure their employees wouldn't starve, but the same couldn't be said for any of the ruin rats. Based on the contents of this missive, she had no way to guess when trading might resume again.

The voices grew closer, and she quickly closed the terminal. Leo grabbed her arm and they scooted deeper into the shadows. They ducked behind some crates just in time for the door to open.

Light shone from the outside hallway, and she waited, hoping whoever had entered would keep moving. Someone hummed a wordless tune, and the sound of some crates being opened nearby caused her heart to skip a beat.

"Did you find the spare circuit boards?" a woman asked from somewhere outside the room.

"Nope," came the answering reply from almost directly in front of them. "It looks like these are just the extra food stores. I'll keep my eyes open, but the circuit boards might be in the comm room."

The woman cursed. "Shari's going to be up soon. She wanted me to run a full diagnostic on the system before she got on shift. One of the circuit boards got fried somehow, and I need to install a new one before running it."

Skye tensed. If they ran a diagnostic check while they were still inside the camp, their presence would be detected.

"Did you look in the tech room?"

"That's my next stop," the woman replied with a sigh.

"Let me finish this and I'll come help you look."

"Thanks. We need to get all this shit organized before the boss gets back from the towers."

The man snorted, and Skye cringed as more crates were

moved. It sounded like he was even closer now. "Put Cruncher on it when he wakes up. That's the perfect job for a new recruit."

"You're just a little bit evil," the woman said with a laugh. "Come on and help me find them. It's getting late, and Shari will be up soon."

The door closed, and the sound of footsteps grew dimmer. Skye let out a breath.

"We need to hurry," she whispered, standing and moving back toward the terminal.

Leo nodded. "You keep looking for the surveillance. I'll check the crates to see if there's anything else we can use in here. The food supplies will be a huge help."

"The food crates should be labeled with a red 'F'." Skye said, turning the terminal back on. She quickly began scrolling through the folders searching for the surveillance access. After several more minutes, she located it and quickly disabled the exterior cameras along the same route she'd traveled with Leo. Before they left, she'd drawn a map for Chance so he could drive the transport right up to the front door.

Her fingers flew over the keyboard as she tried to locate the settings controlling the crew's quarters privacy dividers. It might be possible to trigger them to lock, which would buy them some additional time. They'd still need to avoid the people who were awake, but it would limit their potential for getting caught.

"We good?" Leo whispered, taking a step toward her.

Skye nodded, hoping no one woke up earlier than normal. Her efforts at locking them inside their quarters could easily be reversed, but it would take at least ten minutes.

"We're ready to send the signal, but it sounds like the supplies are scattered throughout the camp." She checked the time. "We're still okay, but we can't afford any more delays. We have to grab what we can and run."

"Can you find out where they store medical supplies?"

"I'll try," she said, turning back to the terminal and opening more folders. She quickly scanned through pages of worthless notes. "Most are going to be stored in the medical room. That's near the front of the camp, but the excess should be in the storeroom. OmniLab labels the crates with a blue 'M'."

"What about equipment?"

"Orange 'T' for tech," she said, still searching through notes. "We won't know the contents until we open each one." She muttered a curse under her breath. "I can't find a detailed list. It's too disorganized. I think the food and medical supplies need to be a priority. We can always go low-tech until trading starts up again, but the other items are necessities."

"I'm sending the signal now," Leo said, pulling out the commlink and entering a command. He slipped it back into his pocket and motioned toward the door. "Chance will be here in a few minutes. I need to get back to the entrance to show him where the supplies are located."

"Let's go," she said, following right behind him.

Leo opened the door and looked outside before gesturing for her to follow him. They headed back down the hall toward the direction of the tech room. The door was closed, but she could hear at least three people inside talking.

Leaning close to Leo, she whispered, "Go meet up with Chance. I'll disable the comms and meet you in the medical room."

Leo nodded and quietly moved down the hall in the direction of the exit. With her heart pounding in her chest, Skye approached the communication room. The door was shut, but she didn't hear anything. She gripped her knife tightly, hoping she wouldn't need to use it.

Skye opened the door and relaxed slightly. It was empty. One of the people they'd overheard earlier must have been assigned to man the communication system. She quickly headed to the console to find they were still logged in. Her luck was continuing to hold. Entering several commands, she quickly disrupted their communication devices. Even if someone woke up now and found themselves locked inside the crew's quarters, they wouldn't be able to call out using their commlinks.

Slipping back out of the room, Skye headed toward the tech room where people were working. She pried off the panel cover to the door and crossed the wiring. With a snap and hiss, the wiring sparked. They'd be locked inside the room for a short time until they rewired it, but that was all her crew needed.

Skye darted down the hall in the direction of the medical room. Unless someone was actively being treated, this room was usually empty. Two medical beds, cabinets, and a host of other equipment was nearby waiting for the camp's next emergency. Skye grabbed an empty box and put it on one of the beds. Sorting through the nearby drawers, she tossed a bunch of items into the box and started searching the cabinets.

The door opened, and her hand immediately went to her knife. At the sight of Leo, she relaxed and motioned toward the box.

"That box is ready to go. I'll fill another and disconnect one of their bone molds. We may have three people still moving throughout the camp, so tell Chance and everyone to be careful. I've locked down the tech room."

"Got it," Leo said, picking up the box she'd put on the bed. "They just pulled up. I told them where the food was located, and they're going to grab some of those crates and whatever else they can find."

She nodded and went back to work unceremoniously grabbing medicine, bandages, and other medical supplies.

When she finished, she quickly unhooked one of the bone molds from the wall while Leo came back to grab the second box. The items they were stealing wouldn't affect those living within the Omni trading camp, but they could completely change the lives of the ruin rats. Even so, Skye tried to bury her guilt. She'd never dream of taking such things from another ruin rat camp. If there were any other option, she'd do it in a heartbeat.

Skye finished filling the last box and carried it out of the medical room. Their time was almost up. At any second, people would either be waking up or they'd figure out how to undo her sabotage. A shout caught her attention, and she ran toward the entrance to see a grisly sight.

A box had fallen to the ground with the contents spilled across the floor. Leo was grappling with a familiar dark-haired man while Wes was on the ground, bleeding heavily from a stomach wound.

"Stop! Bolt, don't hurt him!" Skye dropped her box and rushed over to intervene.

"Stay back, Skye!" Leo ordered, still grappling with Bolt.

She ignored him, unwilling to allow her former campmate to hurt the man she loved. "Please, Bolt! Let him go!"

Bolt's eyes widened at the sight of her, and his hesitation allowed Leo to gain the upper hand. Leo slammed Bolt against the wall, but Bolt's gaze never left her. The weapon he'd been holding clattered to the ground, and she scooped it up. It was one of the handheld laser pistols designed to stun and subdue. Each trading camp had a few, but they usually kept them locked up unless the alarms were triggered. She held it out, aiming toward Bolt.

Bolt stared at her in shock. "Skye? This was your doing? Why?"

She couldn't help but flinch at the look of betrayal on his face. "I'm sorry, Bolt. We were desperate."

Chance and Mack ran into the hallway carrying boxes of food. Chance swore and dropped the box on the ground and rushed toward Wes. "Mack, get those boxes to the cargo vehicle. Hurry."

Mack hesitated for only a second before Leo snapped, "Now, boy. Move."

She continued holding the weapon tightly, glancing over at Chance and Leo as they bent down to check on Wes. "Is he okay?"

Leo shook his head and looked up at her with an apology in his eyes. "I'm sorry, Skye. It's too late. He's gone." Leo stood and gestured to the boxes on the ground. "Chance, help grab the rest of the boxes. We need to hurry."

Skye swallowed, her heart clenching at the senseless loss of another life. They needed to minimize the dangers to anyone else. Turning back to Bolt, she asked, "How many people are awake right now?"

Bolt frowned at her. "Why should I tell you anything? We trusted you, Skye. You brought them here to attack us?"

"Please, Bolt. No one else needs to get hurt," she said, mentally willing them to hurry. Chance and Leo picked up the boxes on the ground and headed out to the cargo vehicle just as Mack came back in. He started grabbing the items that had scattered on the floor, tossing them back into a box.

"Mom?" Veridian's tentative voice came from the doorway.

Panic flooded through her. Without moving the weapon away from Bolt, she tried to angle herself to prevent Veridian from seeing Wes's body. "Go back to the transport, Veridian. Now."

"Oh, fuck," Bolt muttered, gaping at Veridian. "You were telling the truth. He's Tyler's boy, isn't he?"

Veridian's eyes widened, and he halted in his tracks. "You knew my dad?"

Bolt glanced at her before turning back to Veridian. "Yeah. I worked with him and your mom a long time ago. He's a good guy, your dad."

Skye's heart clenched as her past and present collided, but she didn't lower the weapon. Whatever friendship she'd had with Bolt had disappeared the moment she'd left the trading camp. Even if she'd once liked him, she wasn't sure of his intentions now, especially not when it came to her son.

Veridian took a step forward, caught sight of Wes's body on the ground, and paled. "He's dead, isn't he?"

Unwilling to let the conversation continue, she took a deep breath. "Veridian, please go back to the transport and wait for me there."

Veridian hesitated for a moment, indecision warring on his face. Leo approached him from behind and snapped, "Now, V. Your mom told you to go."

Without another word, Veridian turned and ran back toward the vehicle.

"Shit, Skye, I'm sorry," Bolt said, his expression clearly conflicted. "We didn't know what to think when Philip threw you out of here. He said you were making up stories, but none of us knew what really happened. Why didn't you come talk to me?"

She let out a forced laugh. "What could you have done? What could *anyone* have done?"

"Tyler doesn't know?"

She shook her head. "I tried to go to the towers to tell him, but they threw me out."

"Shit. I'm sorry, Skye." Bolt rubbed the back of his neck. "I can't believe this. He looks just like Tyler."

She managed a weak smile. "I know. Veridian's my reason for everything I've done here tonight. I'm just sorry this had to happen in the first place."

Bolt frowned. "You're here because they shut down trading, aren't you?"

She nodded. "Yes, but I don't want to hurt you or anyone else. We just want to take the few supplies we've collected and leave. Will you allow us to do that?"

Leo took a step toward her. "Skye, I don't think—"

She shook her head. "Bolt, please. You *know* me. We didn't come here tonight to hurt anyone. Outside of Tyler, you were my closest friend. Please don't make me use this on you."

Bolt squeezed his eyes shut and didn't answer. She took a step toward him. "If I lower the weapon, are you going to sound the alarm?"

Bolt lifted his head and glanced toward the garage again. Mack and Chance had finished collecting the rest of the boxes, but Leo hadn't budged. After a long moment, Bolt shook his head. "Go. Get out of here. I'll give you ten minutes to escape before I hit the alarm."

Tears sprung to her eyes, and her hands shook as she lowered the weapon. Walking over to Bolt, she kissed his cheek. "For what it's worth, thank you."

He hugged her. "Just take care of yourself and that kid. And make sure you keep him the hell away from here. No one else in this camp knows you, Skye. I'm the only one left."

She swallowed and nodded, offering him the weapon. "I won't come back. Take care of yourself, Bolt."

He accepted it and slid it into his pocket. "You too, Skye. Be safe."

Leo put his hand on her lower back. "Let's go."

Giving Bolt one more grateful smile, Skye turned her back on the trading camp and walked away one last time.

CHAPTER ELEVEN

SKYE PULLED BACK on the throttle of Wes's speeder, following closely behind the transport carrying Chance and the children. Leo was riding on his speeder beside her, and he kept checking behind them for any signs of pursuit. So far, they hadn't seen any sign of the trader's crew, and it was reassuring to know Bolt had kept his word.

They'd been driving for almost two hours, making sure to cover their tracks so nothing could be traced back to them and lead anyone to Daryl's camp. The supplies they'd acquired would assure her and Veridian of at least another year of living within the camp. But it was going to be an uphill battle fighting for Kayla's right to remain.

She didn't believe Daryl would agree to it, but Leo had asked her to trust him. She did trust him, even if a part of her was already making a contingency plan. This time, she would hold some items in reserve—including a speeder. If necessary, she'd try to convince Leo to leave with her. Together, they could start over. She was pretty sure Chance and Alanza would come too, and Niko if they managed to get the medical supplies back to him in time. She just wished Wes hadn't lost his life in the process of trying to help them survive.

Skye caught sight of the building which housed Daryl's camp. It felt as though a lifetime had passed since she'd left. Lives had been lost, and new bonds had been forged. She wasn't sure she could forgive Daryl for what he'd done. She might understand his reasoning, but it didn't make it right. It's in the most desperate moments that someone learns the depth of their strength. Daryl had proven to be weak, and his decision had destroyed any lingering respect she might have had for him.

Pulling up beside the transport, Skye climbed off the speeder and waited while Chance backed his vehicle in as close to the entrance as possible. One day soon, she'd get both children their own sets of UV gear. They'd proven themselves and their ability to handle difficult situations over the past week. It was time they started their scavenger training. It would be several more years before they were able to go into the ruins on their own, but she intended to make sure they were ready.

Skye climbed into the back of the transport where the children were sitting with the stolen supplies. She pulled off Wes's ill-fitting helmet. "You guys okay?"

Veridian frowned. "We're back at Daryl's camp?"

"Is he going to make us go back to the family camp again?" Kayla asked, mirroring Veridian's worried expression.

Skye crouched down in front of them and took their hands. "We're a team, right?"

When they both nodded, Skye managed a smile. "If he doesn't want us to stay, screw him. We've proven we can accomplish anything together. Besides, we have a bunch of supplies we can use to start over. No matter what, we're going to be okay."

The children exchanged a look, but their shoulders

relaxed. Skye's smile deepened, and she motioned for them to climb out. She glanced over at Leo who was speaking quietly with Chance. Mack was standing nearby, looking somewhat unsure but attentively listening to everything Leo was saying.

Leo met her gaze and walked over to her. "You ready to do this?"

She nodded, gathered the children, and followed him into Daryl's camp with Chance and Mack trailing behind them.

The moment they entered, they were greeted by a not-so-friendly face. Daryl was waiting at the entrance. Alanza was a few steps behind him and rushed toward them.

The young woman smiled brightly at Skye and hugged Veridian tightly. "You're safe! We've all missed you. The camp's been so empty without all of you."

Skye smiled. "We missed you too. How's Niko?"

Alanza lowered her gaze. "If you want to say goodbye, you should do it now. He's barely holding on."

Skye walked over to Alanza and hugged her. Leaning in close, Skye whispered into her ear, "Go outside. There's a bone mold and some other medical equipment that might help Niko. Take what you need for him. I'll be in soon to check on you."

Hope shone in Alanza's eyes, and she nodded. Skye smiled at her and squeezed her hand. "Can you keep an eye on the kids while we talk to Daryl?"

"Of course," Alanza agreed, taking Kayla and Veridian's hands. "Come on, guys. Show me what you have out here."

"Leo," Daryl said sharply, his brow pinched with disapproval. "I want some answers. What the hell is Kayla doing back here? And you've brought me *another* kid?"

"You'll get your answers," Leo retorted, heading down the hall toward Daryl's office without waiting for a response. Skye arched her brow but followed Leo, somewhat amused at the approach he was taking.

Heading over to a nearby crate in Daryl's makeshift office, she perched on the edge of it. Daryl waited until Leo, Chance, and Mack were inside before crossing his arms over his chest and nodding toward Mack.

"Who's the boy?"

Mack scowled. "I'm not a boy. The name's Mack, and I'm a scavenger."

Daryl scanned him up and down. "Not looking for scavengers without experience. You get some first, then come back and talk to me."

Leo strode forward. "You're not the one leading this conversation, Daryl. We came here to give you an option. If you decide not to take it, we walk back out the door."

Daryl arched his brow. "Is that supposed to intimidate me?"

Chance cleared his throat. "You might want to hear Leo out."

Daryl narrowed his eyes at Chance. "If you have a problem with how I run things, you know where to find the exit."

Skye had had enough. She straightened and pushed off the crate. "Watch it, Daryl. I had reservations about even taking this opportunity to you, but Leo wanted to give you a chance first."

Leo walked over to her and put his hand on her lower back in a reassuring gesture. She'd agreed to let Leo take the lead, but she'd be damned if she was going to allow Daryl to bully him. Forcing her body to relax, she clenched her jaw and remained silent while Leo addressed their camp leader.

"In the transport outside, we have enough supplies to feed this camp for the next six months."

Daryl froze, his eyes widening a fraction. "How did you manage that?"

"We also have enough medical supplies and equipment to last at least a year, maybe longer if we're conservative."

Daryl's brow furrowed, and he darted his gaze back and forth between all of them. "What the fuck did you do?"

"We stole them from a trading camp," Leo admitted, and Chance chuckled.

"Are you crazy?!" Daryl shouted, his face turning red. "You're going to get us all killed! They're going to track those supplies, and I won't protect you when they come here. You're out of line."

"They won't track them," Leo said, crossing his arms over his chest. "You may have abandoned Skye when she needed you, but not everyone did. It was with her contacts and knowledge that this was even possible."

Daryl's eyes focused on her. "So *you're* responsible for this latest fuck up?"

"Watch it," Leo snapped, taking a threatening step toward Daryl. "You were right. Trading is suspended for the foreseeable future because the leader of the Omni Towers was killed. None of us know how long we're going to be without supplies. If you want a bite of what we have to offer, you're going to shut up and listen."

Daryl's expression hardened, but he inclined his head. "I'm listening."

"This is how it's going to be: you're going to step down as camp leader in the next six months. During that time, I expect you to slowly turn over the reins to me. In exchange, you'll be allowed to stay here to help oversee the day-to-day camp activities. But the final decision about who's going to remain in this camp will be solely up to me."

Daryl scoffed. "You can't think I'm going to go along with this. If this is about keeping Skye and Veridian here, I've already agreed, provided she can keep covering the boy's expenses. But I will not have another child here. You'll burn through those supplies in record time if you want to go along with this foolishness."

"This isn't a negotiation," Leo said sharply. "I'm telling you what the terms will be. Otherwise, I will walk out of this camp and take everyone with me who wants to go. How many of them are going to stick by your side in a dying camp?"

"All of them, if they want to survive after those supplies run out. You don't have the experience to run this place."

"You're right," Skye agreed, moving to stand beside Leo once more. "You have a lot of experience in running the camp, but Leo's got something you don't: the respect of everyone here and the willingness to take risks."

Daryl glared at her. "You're going to take him down with you, and why? For a kid who's not even yours?"

"Kayla will be my responsibility, not Skye's," Leo announced in a firm voice.

She stared up at Leo in shock. "Leo, I can't ask—"

"No," he said, interrupting her and taking her hand. He gave it a light squeeze and added, "I told you, we're in this together. You're not going to walk away from Kayla, and I'm not walking away from you. If she's important to you, she stays."

Skye's eyes filled with moisture, and she nodded.

Daryl sighed. "You both have lost your minds. Fine. The girl can stay."

Leo gestured toward Mack. "Mack will also be staying on as a scavenger. I'll show him the ropes, but he should be up and running in a few weeks."

Daryl gave him a look of disgust. "Is there any point in arguing?"

"No," Leo replied.

Skye lowered her gaze and bit back a smile.

"Well, since that's all settled," Chance clapped Mack on

the shoulder, "welcome to the camp. Now, why don't you help me start unloading those supplies? Afterward, I'll show you around."

They headed out of the room, and Skye turned back to Leo. An overwhelming surge of love and pride filled her at everything he'd accomplished. He'd be a great camp leader, and if it happened sooner than they expected, they'd all adapt. He met her gaze and leaned down to kiss her.

"I'm not hiding anything anymore, Skye. You're it for me, and I don't care who knows it."

She smiled up at him, and his gaze softened. He ran his thumb over her cheek and murmured, "Those fucking dimples of yours. They did me in the moment I first saw you smile."

Her smile deepened. It was tempting to thank Leo in a more personal manner, but he still needed to finish ironing out the details with Daryl. "I'll go check on the kids while you're finishing up in here." She leaned close and whispered, "Come find me when you're done."

"It's a promise," he said, squeezing her hand again before releasing her.

With one last smile, she turned and left Daryl's office. Heading back down the hall, she stopped outside the room where Niko had been moved. Alanza and Pepper, another one of their scavengers, were sitting on the floor together unpacking some of the medical supplies. They'd already hooked up the bone mold to one of Niko's legs. Once it had been corrected, they'd switch and do the other one. But it was obvious they'd been busy. Niko was sleeping, but his color was already looking better than it had been when she'd left for the family camp.

Alanza looked at Skye with tears in her eyes. She jumped up and embraced her. "How can I ever thank you? He actually has a chance now."

Skye returned her hug. "You don't ever have to thank me for this, Alanza. We all love Niko. I'm just glad we got here in time with those supplies."

Alanza sniffed and nodded, wiping away her tears. Skye looked over to see Veridian sitting on the floor beside Pepper and Niko. He was busy talking around the nutrient bar in his mouth and telling Pepper about the past week.

Skye frowned. "Where's Kayla?"

Alanza gestured toward the hallway. "She went to use the bathroom. She should be back in a minute."

Skye nodded. "I'll go check on her."

Leaving Veridian still chatting away with them, she headed back down the hall. The bathroom area was empty, so she continued walking, searching for any sign of Kayla. Chance started to pass her, carrying another large box.

"Hey, did you see Kayla?"

"Yeah, she's outside. I told her to stay out of the way while we're bringing in the supplies."

Skye arched her brow, wondering why Kayla had gone off on her own. "I'll find her. Thanks."

Outside, the early morning light was almost blinding. The UV guard at the front entrance blocked the most harmful rays, but it wasn't a good idea to linger without protective clothing. She spotted Kayla standing near one of the speeders, staring off across the landscape.

Walking over toward the young girl, Skye ran her hand over Kayla's dark hair. "Hey. What are you doing out here, sweetheart?"

"Saying goodbye," Kayla whispered, still staring in the direction of the ruined city.

Skye paused, a small frown crossing her face. "You don't need to say goodbye, Kayla. Leo and I spoke with Daryl. We made all the arrangements. You're going to stay here with us."

Kayla nodded. "I know. The voice said you and Leo would

protect me until I grow up. I can hear it better when I'm close to the ruins, but it's tired now. It's going back to sleep, and I won't hear it again for a long time."

Skye froze, trying to understand what Kayla was telling her. It should have been impossible, but some part of her knew what Kayla said was real. Crouching down beside Kayla, she stared in the same direction—where the chasm was located. Skye swallowed, trying to bury her unease. A voice had guided her in the ruins—finding Kayla was proof of that —and now a voice was speaking to Kayla.

Skye turned back to Kayla. "Will you tell me about the voice?"

Kayla frowned and glanced over at her. "We're not supposed to talk about it. No one else will understand. We're supposed to forget. It's safer that way."

"Leo didn't hear it," Skye said quietly. "Do you know why?"

"He's not like us," Kayla explained. "You're special like me. The voice said you can hide me from them until it's time. That's your gift and your power. But we can't tell anyone."

The hair on the back of Skye's neck stood on end. Kayla's words had the resonance of truth, and a sneaking suspicion entered Skye's mind. She stared back out across the landscape, both in the direction of the chasm and of something much more dangerous. She already knew the answer, but the question still needed to be asked.

"Who am I hiding you from?"

Kayla frowned, her eyes shining with tears. "From the people in the towers. They want to hurt me."

The memory of the powerful storm over a week ago crossed through Skye's mind. The strange greenish hue of the sky had been almost the exact same shade of green of Kayla's eyes.

"Keep her close to you, daughter of the sky," a voice whispered

in her mind. *"She will need your guidance to survive what's to come. Protect her with your life, and she will do the same for those you love —because she will love them in return."*

"I will," Skye promised, reaching down to take Kayla's hand in hers. She didn't understand how any of this was possible, but she'd learned that some things needed to be taken on faith. Everything was connected, and Fate always had a plan.

"Come on, sweetheart. If we're going to turn you and Veridian into the best scavenging team possible, we should get started."

"Really?"

"Mmhmm." Skye led Kayla toward the entrance of the scavenging camp. "Leo and I are going to make sure of it."

ABOUT THE AUTHOR

Jamie A. Waters is an award-winning science fiction and paranormal romance author. Her first novel, Beneath the Fallen City (previously titled as The Two Towers), was a winner of the Readers' Favorite Award in Science-Fiction Romance and the CIPA EVVY Award in Science-Fiction.

Jamie currently resides in Florida with her two neurotic dogs who enjoy stealing socks and chasing lizards. When she's not pursuing her passion of writing, she's usually trying to learn new and interesting random things (like how to pick locks or use the self-cleaning feature of the oven without setting off the fire alarm). In her downtime, she enjoys reading, playing computer games, painting, or acting as a referee between the dragons and fairies currently at war inside her closet.

You can learn more by visiting: www.jamieawaters.com

CPSIA information can be obtained
at www.ICGtesting.com
Printed in the USA
LVHW112345200819
628405LV00001B/111/P